GUT-SHOT GUNMAN

"It's a long story and it ain't as if you'll get to remember any of it. Let's just say you should have stayed in Denver. I got nothing personal against you, my ownself. But the gent I worked for says lawmen like you ought to be stomped out, lest they multiply."

Longarm shrugged and kept walking . . .

The hired gun said, "Oh, I reckon this is about far enough."

Longarm turned around with a resigned smile, and as soon as he was facing the son of a bitch, let him have both barrels of his derringer.

Longarm hunkered down beside him to see what his two derringer slugs had wrought as he explained, pleasantly, "I'm sorry I gut-shot you. But it was your own fault, making me palm my belly gun left-handed. I'd have nailed you clean at that range if I'd been shooting right-handed. But don't cry too much. It won't hurt you in a few minutes."

TABOR EVANS

LONGARM

AND THE UTAH KILLERS

JOVE BOOKS, NEW YORK

LONGARM AND THE UTAH KILLERS

A Jove Book / published by arrangement with
the author

PRINTING HISTORY
Jove edition / April 1988

ISBN: 0-515-09520-6

Jove books are published by The Berkley Publishing Group,
200 Madison Avenue, New York, New York 10016.
The name "JOVE" and the "J" logo
are trademarks belonging to Jove Publications, Inc.

PRINTED IN THE UNITED STATES OF AMERICA

10 9 8 7 6 5 4 3 2 1

Chapter 1

The bearded man in the grime-glazed buckskin shirt moved clear of the bar as he morosely warned Longarm, "Never marry no woman who empties your ashtray whilst you're still smoking." Then he went for his gun.

Longarm had expected he might, and things proceeded to get confusing and noisy as hell in the Parthenon Saloon for a spell. As the last reverberations of Longarm's .44-40 faded away and the gunsmoke began to clear, surviving patrons and hired help gingerly peered out from such cover as they'd found to find the tall Deputy U.S. Marshal Custis Long still on his feet, reloading his six-gun. The same could not be said for the stranger who'd been imprudent enough to slap leather against the man known far and wide, with mingled fear and admiration, as Longarm. For as the result of his foolishness the unwashed as well as sinister stranger now lay spread-eagle on his back, soaking into the sawdust pretty good. The three neat holes Longarm had punched through the front of his glazed buckskin shirt

1

weren't bleeding much. But as most of the crowd knew, a .40-44 slug seldom comes out the back of a man as neatly as it goes in his front.

The gent on the floor should have been dead. So even Longarm was a mite startled when he opened one eye to stare up at the pressed-tin ceiling to continue, in a surprisingly conversational tone: "I should have known what she was when she done that the first evening I come courting, at a time when most females are on their very best behavior. But the sage gent who first said a stiff dong has no conscience forgot to add that it ain't really peering into the future all that much, neither. All I had on my poor feverish mind before I won her hand in marriage was how nice she looked and smelt. How was I to know she took a bath every goddamned day of the year?"

Then he just went on staring up at—or maybe through —the ceiling with his grizzled jaw sort of slack. Longarm put his reloaded sidearm back in its cross-draw holster under his tobacco-brown tweed coat and hunkered down to feel the side of the downed man's throat as, somewhere out on the streets of Denver, a police whistle commenced to chirp.

Feeling no pulse, Longarm rose once more to his substantial full height as the barkeep leaned far across the mahogany for a clearer view, muttering, "Damn it, Longarm. Nobody ain't supposed to start gunfights in this sedate part of town."

Longarm nodded soberly and replied, "Such goings-on are sort of frowned on west of Larimer Street, since the state capital got all gussied up with asphalt paving, street lamps, and such. You have my word I only stepped in for some needled beer after an honest day's toil over at the federal building, Doc. I'd have come in more cautious and polite if I'd known this poor cuss was on your premises."

The Denver beat-cop coming through the bat-wings from the street must have known the way it was done, too. For he had his own revolver out and aimed as he started to

2

tell Longarm to stick 'em up, recognized his fellow peace officer, and settled for saying, "I might have known it was you making all that racket on my beat, Longarm." Then he moved in for a closer look at the untidy results of all that noise, whistled, and added, "When you set out to clean a man's plow you don't mess around, do you? I know you're as amiable a cuss as Marshal Billy Vail has working for him, these days. So is it safe to assume that poor drifter took offense at that tweed suit and shoestring tie they make you boys wears about the federal building?"

Longarm shook his head and said, "Hell, I ain't *that* neat. The gent at our feet was wanted on a federal murder charge. I only figured who he had to be when I saw him start to get murderous with me, just now. He must have recognized me, first, as the law, and the results you see before you."

Longarm reached under his frock coat to fish a cheroot from a vest pocket as he added, "It's just as well it ended this way, I reckon. But if ever a man deserved a hanging, a slow one, he had to be it. His name was Andrew MacTavish. He was the BIA agent on the Arapaho reserve to the southeast. The lady he murdered, with his fists, was his wife, Rosemary. He made it federal by beating her to death on federal property with a mess of federal wards witnessing the crime. The Arapaho say he chased her out of their house, already beaten bloody, and finished her off in their dooryard, pounding her head all out of shape as he sat on her chest. The way we put it together, she was one of them fussy housekeepers while he, as anyone can see, was a natural slob. They'd been married nearly seven years when he just sort of snapped one evening, I reckon."

Another man who'd only come in for a beer and wound up with sawdust all over his black wool duds observed, "I can see what he was bitching about at the last, then. I had a wife like that one time, back east. That's why I come out west. I have to allow you done what you thought you had to, Longarm. But it's still a crying shame how women take

3

advantage of us poor brutes. The one I got trapped by never said a thing about my cigars or fingernails until we was on our honeymoon. Next thing I knew it was a choice between giving up smoking or sleeping on the sofa. Then, even when she got me to quit smoking and take a hot bath before we went to bed, the cruel gal took to having herself a headache almost every night."

Longarm lit his own somewhat pungent three-for-a-nickel smoke before he observed, "I can see why you left her. The point is that you managed to refrain from killing her. That's the one and mighty important difference that separates gents I have to arrest from those I don't. Show me a man who's never wanted to clobber a pesky woman and I'll show you a born sissy. It's just a law of nature that when a couple is courting the male is hoping his little darling will stay as sweet as she is, while the meantime, the female is hoping to change him into the man she'd been planning to marry up with, if such a freak of nature ever came down the pike."

He blew a thoughtful smoke ring and sadly added, "It's the law of the land that neither is allowed to murder the other *when,* not *if,* both wind up disappointed with the way things naturally work out. That's one of the reasons I'm still single. What both you and the late MacTavish said about the way gals act, up to that fatal moment when the preacher says it's too late to ride on, is all too true."

He glanced at the door to observe that while lots of curious faces were peering in from outside, none of them were wearing the Yankee blue of the Denver PD. He turned to the one copper badge who'd seen fit to investigate and said, "Well, I got to get it on down the road, pard. If you'll be kind enough to tidy up here, I'll have our office boy type up a full statement in triplicate for Denver, come morning when the office is open."

The beat-cop shook his head stubbornly and said, "Not hardly, Longarm. You can't just gun a man down in downtown Denver and walk away from the results."

4

Longarm swore softly and replied, "I knew this town was going to the dogs when they changed its name from Cherry Creek. I just now told you everything you really have to have for the desk sergeant's blotter at your precinct house. All the big shots we both work for have gone home for the night by now. Come sunrise the powers that be can go over your preliminary report and pick all the nits they like. There's no sense confusing 'em with more details until they ask for 'em, is there?"

The beat-cop's head was shaking some more and Longarm could tell by the stubborn set of the lawman's jaw that either Miss Morgana Floyd or Marshal Billy Vail was going to wind up mad as hell at him, no matter how this worked out. Miss Morgana had told him to pick her up at the orphan asylum when she got off at seven, which hardly seemed possible if Denver PD aimed to make such a fuss about one dead fugitive. On the other hand, old Billy Vail was even less likely to forgive him if he beat up on a local peace officer, and this particular one wasn't about to let him leave without a struggle.

Longarm glanced up at the clock above the bar, winced as he saw how much time he had left to work with, and then stepped over to the bar with a resigned shrug and ordered that needled beer he'd come in for in the first damned place.

That encouraged others to do the same and so, as he'd sort of hoped, the dead man and over-eager beat-cop were left out in the middle of the floor to stare at one another, if that was the fool beat-cop's notion of a way to spend an evening, with the rest of the town about to get more interesting.

It didn't work. Longarm hoped against hope to be sort of overlooked in the general confusion by the time the morgue wagon and some more copper badges showed up. But though he hunkered down over his beer schooner and didn't watch, the officious bastards soon had the cadaver wrapped in a rubberized canvas tarp and on its way outside. Then the first pain-in-the-ass beat-cop came over with a police sergeant Longarm had never drunk with to tell him, "You can ride with us in the meat wagon. Once we get your victim to the morgue it's only a short walk to headquarters and you can tell your side to the night officer."

Longarm growled, "Bite your tongue. That rascal wasn't nobody's *victim*. I told you we've got an outstanding murder warrant on him and, even if we didn't, he was the one who started it."

The sergeant said, less rudely but as firmly, "That's one of the things our own brass will want to go into with you, Deputy. You have a copy of that Wanted flier on you, I hope?"

Longarm swore under his breath before he replied, "Sure I do. In my head. Do you think I have room in my fool pockets for all the damned wires and posters we get every time we turn around?"

He tapped the side of his skull with a finger, explaining, "I got hundreds of faces and the dozen or so names that go with each, up here. I can't get at the official paper out on old MacTavish until my office opens in the morning. So, like I said, I see no reason to waste half the night on paperwork that'll only have to be done over again, tomorrow. That old boy I shot will smell no worse by then, unless the morgue's run out of ice of late. You boys go on, if you want. I'd just now started another beer and—"

"We'll wait," cut in the police sergeant, politely but firmly.

So Longarm muttered, "Shit," swallowed less than half the contents of the schooner, and slammed it back down, saying, "I'd just as soon get it over with. I hope you boys understand that this is on my own time."

The sergeant nodded with some sympathy, but pointed out, "You were on your own time when you gunned the poor cuss. Let's go. I doubt you'll be held up at headquarters more than a few hours."

6

Longarm went with them. Billy Vail would never understand him pistol-whipping *two* cops. So there was nothing else a man with a more serious place to be could do. It was still light outside, damn the summer sun at this latitude, so the wrapped-up cadaver was plainly visible as the three of them sat on the tailgate and the morgue wagon got to rolling under them. As they swung a corner to head west the body shifted just enough to let some fumes escape from its rubberized wrapping. The sergeant grimaced and said, "Jesus, he can't have been dead *that* long."

Longarm shrugged and explained, "He murdered his wife because she made him wash up a lot. That was a good six weeks ago, and he might not have killed her if he liked to bathe and shave. That was how I recognized him, just in time. It takes dedication to get *that* disgusting in only six weeks."

The other copper sniffed, wrinkled his nose in disgust, and said, "Nobody can stink that bad by just avoiding soap and water a spell. Do you reckon it could be something he ate?"

"I'd say it's mostly his gallbladder you're so vexed about," Longarm said. "One of my rounds took him a mite low, through the guts. That eye-watering part is ammonia. He'd likely pissed his pants, or worse, before I shot him, I mean, and the fresh urine added to the dried crud in them greasy wool pants—"

"Cut it out, I'm fixing to puke," snapped the sergeant. Then he added, as if to himself, "Gallbladder, eh? I always sort of wondered about that, during the war. Sometimes an old boy could just lay there, taking days to get ripe, while others stunk to high heaven the first damned day."

Longarm didn't answer. He didn't like to talk about the war or a teenager from West-by-God-Virginia who'd joined up, expecting it to be a grand adventure, until he got to grow up, fast, at a place called Shiloh. When asked about his misspent youth, Longarm had learned to tell folk he disremembered which side he'd ridden for. It hadn't been all that long ago and a lot of men who did remember, with some bitterness, were still around. The only good thing about those grim times, if one wanted to say anything about it had been good, was that by the time it was over Longarm had learned more about gunfighting than anyone could possibly learn any other way. And, since that first hot summer campaign, the smell of torn-open guts and rotting flesh didn't seem to bother him as much as it did most folk. He'd never learned to *like* death's rotten breath. But since the last time he'd been pinned down on a real battlefield with a whole damned army dead or dying all around him, he'd never seen or smelled anything as disgusting. So maybe a war was good training for a man in his line of work, after all.

The sun was setting behind the front range of the nearby Rockies, but the sky was still lit up inconvenient as hell when they finally reached the morgue, down by the railroad yards. It could have been worse. Miss Morgana Floyd worked at the orphan asylum in Arvada, even farther to the west. So the wagon ride had him almost halfway there, at least.

He got out his watch, swore, and tucked it back in his vest pocket. If he left this very minute he just might make it. He figured the pretty little thing would wait maybe half an hour before she got steamed enough to hail a hansom and go on home alone, mad as a wet hen. Longarm knew where she lived, of course. But the last time he'd come calling after standing her up she'd dumped a washbasin of water out her window on him. He *hoped* it had been a washbasin. No matter how pissed off a gal might be, it hardly seemed possible she'd fill a chamber pot so full *that* early.

The three of them dropped off so that the morgue crew could unload what was left of MacTavish. Longarm told the sergeant he'd wait in the dinky beer joint just down the way. The copper shook his head and said, "Not hardly. You'd know more about the disgusting condition you left

8

him in than I would, and they may want to ask some questions inside."

Longarm shrugged and started to reach for another cheroot. But at three for a nickel a man couldn't afford to throw one away half-smoked, and he knew what tobacco smoke mixed with the reek of death tasted like.

As he followed the litter bearers inside, flanked by the two pesky copper badges, he saw he'd been right about that cheroot. They were too tidy to let dead folk just rot. But the eye-watering fumes of formaldehyde and pine oil disinfectant hardly inspired one to inhale deeply.

The corridor was dimly lit by those newfangled Edison lamps. Longarm knew they cost way too much for the feeble glow they gave off, and it took at least a small steam engine, along with the coal it ate, to get them to glow at all. They likely feared the effects of naked flame on the chemical fumes. Formaldehyde was a poisonous kissing cousin to alcohol when you studied on it.

A morgue attendant who came down the corridor to meet them proved his own nose was as sensitive as Longarm's by sniffing, sighing, and muttering, "Gut shot, eh? All right, let's put it on ice with the other stiffs and shut the door tight. The forensic crew just knocked off for the day. So the autopsy will have to wait until morning. I wish you'd brought this one in a little sooner. A gut-shot stiff smells a lot better once they haul out the mess and hose out the body cavity."

The beat-cop gagged and said something about waiting for Longarm and the sergeant out front. Then he headed for the street exit a lot faster than he'd come in. But the sergeant, cuss his hide, was made of sterner stuff. Longarm decided it was just as well when he noticed the morgue crew were asking him all the questions and that he was doing all the answering. None of the questions were all that tough. The night crew's job was to just hang on to dead bodies until somebody more important got to worry about how they wound up dead.

The cold, clammy, and windowless storage bay they wound up in was no longer cooled by real ice, of course. A city morgue in a city that rated a uniformed police force and street paving tended to keep up to date. So, while everyone still called it putting them on ice, from force of habit, the cold storage bay was in truth kept cool by frost-covered brine pipes running the length of one wall. The colder-than-ice liquid was pumped from another newfangled machine on the roof, most likely. Longarm had read about such notions, though he wasn't sure how it worked, and considered the prediction that someday they'd get them small enough for private homes to use instead of iceboxes a mite impractical.

But the notion sure worked back here. Outside, it was going on high summer and, in here, a man could see his own breath. Longarm didn't breath all that heavy, though. For despite the cool, the air was mighty pungent. He didn't have to ask why. Anyone could see MacTavish wasn't the first customer they'd had recently. The other bodies lay on slabs, lined up like domino tiles so that the stiffs lay with their feet aimed at the brine pipes and their heads closer to the far wall. You could tell, even though they'd all been covered with white muslin sheets.

The straw boss whipped such a sheet off a vacant slab, patted the cold zinc, and told the others to unwrap the rascal and spread him out neat before rigor mortis made that any tougher. The boys toting the dead killer placed him on yet another vacant slab to do so. Aside from Longarm, who'd already seen what a dead man looked like, everyone sort of gathered around as if they were unwrapping a Christmas surprise. As the remains were exposed to the dim light, the gent in charge whistled and said, "Nice shooting. Who got to drill him like that, you?"

The sergeant half turned to wave a casual hand as he replied, "Nope. It was this federal deputy here."

Then he blinked, gaped all about, and added, "Hey,

10

Longarm? Where the hell did that big moose go? He was *here,* just a second ago."

The straw boss shrugged and said, "He likely had to go puke. That happens a lot around here, even with our own greener hands." Then he told his crew, "Hold him straight as you shift him to this other slab, boys." Then, as they did their best but let the body sag a mite, he shouted, "God-damn it, you're letting him drip, and this floor was mopped only an hour ago!"

The sergeant was more worried about a living body he seemed to be missing. As the morgue crew plopped Mac-Tavish down again and hauled the sheet up over him, the sergeant moved to the doorway to call down the corridor, "Longarm?"

He was joined there by the straw boss, who was bitch-ing, "We could let it go 'til morning if it was just blood. But if the boss comes in to spy black bile and worse on the tiles he'll have a fit. I'd best get our mop jockey to work back here before it dries."

The sergeant wasn't listening. He tore down the corri-dor, out the exit, and slid to a stop when he spotted his junior officer leaning against a lamppost near the morgue wagon. He asked the beat-cop, "Where's Longarm?" and, as he'd feared, the only man in sight replied, "Search me. Wasn't he inside with you, just now, Sarge?"

They got that sorted out soon enough. Then they both went back inside to search high and low. But as the helpful morgue crew told them, there just weren't that many places to look for a live body in a city morgue. Most of the offices were locked up for the night in any case. In the end the sergeant could only call the missing lawman a lot of awful names and add, "We're wasting time here. I knew the ras-cal was anxious to go somewhere else this evening. We'll just hand in our own reports and let the captain worry about the crazy bastard."

And thus it came to pass that less than half an hour later an uneasy young Mexican named Hernando entered the

11

cold storage bin with a mop in one hand and a bucket of pine oil and water in the other, just as Longarm, assuming by now the coast was clear, sat up on the slab he'd been aboard all this time. He'd naturally covered himself with the sheet he'd found on the vacant slab. So from Hernando's point of view a very large corpse was rising from its slab, sheet and all.

Under the sheet, Longarm heard the mop and bucket hit the tile, followed by a softer thud. He sighed, said, "Well, it was worth a try," and hauled off the sheet to see who'd caught him. Then he saw a skinny Mex kid in a white uniform sprawled unconscious on the floor between the tools of his trade. Longarm had to smile. But then he made sure the boy was only in a faint, then dragged him clear of the spilled disinfectant before he put on his hat and simply strolled out to the street.

It was darker outside now. It was *damn it* after seven, too. But he lucked out at a livery just another block west. For the saddle mount they were willing to hire out to him was a good old semi-retired cow pony who didn't mind loping on pavement until, on the far side of the Platte River Bridge, the paving gave way to summer-baked dirt and Longarm could yell, "Powder River and let her buck and move your ass, you infernal snail!"

The cool shades of evening and perhaps some fond childhood memories inspired the old cow pony to move pretty good to begin with. Longarm whipping its rump with his hat made it go even faster. But Arvada was five or more miles west of the Platte, and as he finally reined his lathered mount to a stop in the dooryard of the orphan asylum, Longarm was sure Miss Morgana Floyd was going to hit him with a broom, if she was still there. She'd warned him the last time he'd stood her up that she intended to, and old Morgana was a woman of her word.

But as he entered the front office, marked HEAD MATRON, with a sheepish smile, he saw the pretty little brunette was seated at her desk with her uniform still doing its

12

best to hide her considerable breasts under starched and pleated linen. Before Longarm could say he was sorry she sighed and said *she* was, adding, "I wish they'd let us have one of those newfangled Bell telephones out here, darling. I could have saved you the trip."

"No you couldn't have. Billy Vail don't hold with modern notions, and I couldn't afford one at my furnished digs unless I cut out smoking entirely. But how come you wanted to call me by telephone and tell me not to come out here, honey? I just rode through hell and high water under the distinct impression we had a dinner date in town."

Morgana sighed wistfully and explained, "The matron I'd picked to ride night watch on our dear little bastards came down with chicken pox this afternoon. Don't ever take a job in an orphan asylum if you're not already immune to all the childhood agues you can find in the books. I had to send her into the county hospital, along with a couple of other staff members who confessed *they'd* never had chicken pox, yet."

Longarm hung his battered Stetson on a wall hook and moved over to hook a hip over one corner of her desk, on her side, as he asked, "Couldn't you have put one of your other gals in charge of quarters, seeing as you're the boss lady out here?"

He liked her even more, despite what it was doing to his hopes, when she replied, simply, "I could. But it wouldn't be fair. The other girls have their own lives to lead on their own time. So I make it my habit to post our extra duty roster a month in advance. That way, they can all plan ahead and—"

"I had a first sergeant like that, once," he cut in. "He was one of the few decent top-kicks I ever came across in my army days. Any old soldier can tell you sad tales of pulling guard duty or CQ at the last minute, with no way to tell his gal in town why he wouldn't be by, that evening."

Morgana shot him a keen look and said, "I might have known you were, ah, dropping by on unsuspecting maidens a good fifteen years ago, you brute. Didn't you tell me one time you were only a teenager during the war?"

He grinned down at her and said, "So were the gals I was going out with, in them days. To tell the truth, I like my gals a mite more mature, these days."

She giggled despite herself and said, "It's just as well we never met during the war. For I was only nine years old at the time, and that's a little young for a girl to lose her virginity."

"I was wondering how old you might be, no offense. And speaking of such matters, how late do you reckon we ought to wait tonight before we put out the lamp and lose your virginity some more?"

She shook her head sadly and said, "Please don't tease me, darling. You know full well what I've been saving up for you since you got back to town. But I'm on duty here."

"Don't you have a lock on your door?" he asked.

"You know damned well I do. But you promised, the last time we did it on this very desk, that you'd behave yourself in the future. So this is the future and you have to behave yourself. The dear little bastards I'm in charge of are barely in bed and not likely to go to sleep for hours."

She saw the look in his eyes, read it wrong, and pleaded, "Try to understand, Custis. Some of the poor little things are new at the game of orphanhood. I never know when I may have to comfort one of them. I know they tell us to just let them cry it out. But could you ignore a little boy or girl who's just woke up from a nightmare, bawling for its mother?"

"Nope. Not if I knew said mother was no longer with us. I follow your drift, so let's say no more about it."

She looked down at her desk blotter and murmured, "I'm sorry you rode all that way for nothing. I guess you'll be riding back to town and, well, Sherman Avenue, right?"

Longarm didn't know who might have told Morgana about a certain widow woman up on Capital Hill. Someone always did, cuss 'em. He didn't think it would reassure

Morgana if he said his other old pal was entertaining house guests she didn't want to explain him to. So he got back to his feet and said, "I'd best tend to my mount before he catches a chill. Is it jake with you if I oat and water him in your stable, honey?"

She looked up, blankly, to ask, "Aren't you riding right back to town, Custis?"

"Nope. I fainted a Mex and no doubt made Denver PD mad at me to keep our date. So if I can't take off my pants, the least I can do is keep you company."

Morgana leaped to her feet, threw her arms around him on tiptoe, and kissed him in a way that made the notion of keeping one's pants on downright painful.

His raging erection began to subside by the time he had the livery mount unsaddled, rubbed down, and stalled with a few oats and plenty of water in the stable out back. As he slid the big door shut and turned from the stable he saw he was not alone in the dimly lit yard. The dark figure approaching was a mite small to slap leather on, so Longarm just called out, amiably, "Ain't it past your bedtime, sport?"

A girlish voice replied, "Longarm? What are you doing out here tonight?"

He knew who she was, now. He'd rescued her from a pimp in downtown Denver a spell back. She tended to change her name and age to suit the occasion. But whoever she was and however old she might be, she was way too young for the life she'd been leading, and that was why he'd brought her out here to the orphan asylum in the first place. As she drew close enough for him to make out her elfin features, Longarm said, "I got business out here. You don't. Not out here in the yard, leastways. I thought they put you kids to bed right after supper."

"They do," she said, "and I haven't gotten any screwing since you brung me out here, damn it. That's why I'm leaving."

Longarm said, "Not aboard any of them ponies in the

15

stable, if you've a lick of sense. Like I told you the last time, whoring can get you ninety days in the county jail. The state of Colorado *hangs* you for stealing *horses*. I reckon they consider a horse thief more shocking than even a child whore."

She stamped her foot in the dust and protested, "I'm no such thing, damn it." So he asked, pleasantly, "No such what, a whore or a child?"

"I'm a woman with womanly needs," she said, "and all they let me do out here is study books, sewing, and eating mush. They won't even serve us kids coffee, and I'm just dying for a smoke."

He thought before he decided on, "If I give you a whole cheroot, will you promise to smoke it out here and then go back to bed like a good little girl?"

"I don't want to be a good little girl no more, I've tried it. It's just tedious as hell. I told you when you was bringing me out here that I ain't cut out for this orphan shit."

"I remember," he said. "But as I pointed out at the time, you *are* an orphan, unless you'd like to go home to that disgusting old man you told me you'd run away from, assuming you told me one true word."

She stamped her foot again and insisted, "I don't care what I said then. Getting screwed by grown men is a lot more fun than hanging around with silly little boys who can't get it in."

Longarm whistled softly and asked, "Have you been playing such games with the other orphans out here, sis?"

She sounded almost innocent when she replied, "Sure, screwing is lots of fun. Only most of the kids out here are too shy to even try, and the few I've managed to talk into playing grown-up can't seem to get it right. So far, I haven't found one boy who's hung manly enough to treat a woman right. That's how come I'm lighting out, and you can't stop me."

"Sure I could. But I'm not sure that would help them other orphans much. It would be aiding and abetting if I

16

was to offer you any money or even advice on how to make it back to where I found you. But if you just have to go, I hope you still remember what I told you, before, about the grim things that can happen to a whore who's *big* enough to fight back."

She shrugged and said, "I can take care of myself. I can make it back downtown before midnight, even walking. I only need to talk three or four gents into it and I'll have enough to get a decent breakfast, with real coffee."

Longarm grimaced, nodded soberly, and said, *"Via con Dios,* then, you poor little headstrong slut."

"Aren't you going to try and stop me?"

Longarm shook his head and told her, "I already done that, once. In my line of work you soon learn that wild kids come in two varieties. Some can be reformed. Some just have to run wild until they run out of luck. So run along and peddle your skinny ass 'til somebody busts it for you. Like the Indian chief said, I have spoken."

Then he turned away and headed back for the main building. As he did so the little sass fell in step beside him to ask, "No shit, you don't care if I run off or not?"

"I used to," he said. "I thought you had a brain. I thought a few short years of book-learning and taking baths more regularly might make a decent lady out of you. An asylum is a place that's willing to give you asylum and a break. It ain't a jail. But don't worry if you can't tell the difference, yet. Whores get to spend lots of time in real jails."

They were almost to the back door now. She said, "Well, maybe I ought to wait until the fall roundup before I run off. A gal can make a lot of money, sudden, when the herd's in town."

Longarm opened the back door but barred her entrance, saying, "I ain't sure you ought to stay that long, seeing you've been acting so disgusting with the other kids."

Her voice was almost pleading as she told him, "Hell, I was just bullshitting you. The durned old matrons never give us a chance to even sneak a smoke, and they keep the boys and girls in separate night quarters. Didn't you know that?"

He said, grudgingly, "I told you before, the old gal who runs this place is smart. If I let you back in, will you behave your fool self?"

She said she would and so, having done his duty toward a wayward young gal, Longarm let her in. As she dashed off to get back in bed, Longarm went on to rejoin Morgana and see just how wayward he could get *her,* once things settled down for the night.

It took him until well after ten to get her out of her prim uniform and on the leather chesterfield in her office. She might not have acted so shy if they hadn't had to leave her lamp lit, lest passers-by outside wonder why no light was shining through her drawn window shade. She kept her perky naked breasts covered with her forearms as he undressed, begging him not to look at her and saying other dumb things such as, "You promised the last time not to let this happen again, damn it." Then she laughed like hell as he mounted her, saying, "I'm a man of his word, doll bottom. Anyone can see we ain't doing it on your *desk* this time."

Then they both went too crazy for conversation for a spell. By the time she'd climaxed with him, Morgana had gotten over her shyness. So she got on top, smiling down at him adoringly as she told him, "It's a good thing we never met when I was nine years old. This would have ruined me. But you know I've never been able to say no to you." She began to move atop him as she added, coyly, "Are you sorry we met after I'd had a chance to, ah, get just a little bigger?"

And she didn't know what he was laughing about when he told her, "Nope. I've so far managed to resist the temptations of anyone who ain't full-grown."

Chapter 2

The sage who first decreed that virtue was its own reward had no doubt never messed with the true facts of life all that much. For the next morning, as Longarm strode toward the federal building from the livery, looking satisfied if not all that innocent, he was headed off just east of Larimer by Henry, the prissy young clerk from Billy Vail's office. As they met, Longarm said, "Morning, Henry. Ain't you headed the wrong way?"

Henry shook his head and said, "No. You are. Marshal Vail's had me hunting high and low for you since early last evening. I see he was right about you having spent the night with Madam Gould, after all."

Longarm looked pained and said, "Never mind where I might have spent the night, Henry. What's all the fuss about?"

Henry said, "Denver PD has an arrest warrant out on you. Why on earth did you leave the scene of a crime like that, you fool?"

Longarm considered and replied, "I never left the scene of no crime. I shot the son of a bitch fair and square in the Parthenon, and left in the company of Denver PD. I reckon they may be a mite upset because I couldn't spend the whole damned night with 'em."

Henry sighed and said, "They're hardly a *mite* upset, Longarm. Like I said, they issued an arrest warrant. So now Marshal Vail means to ream your ass good. Only he wants you out of town awhile first, so he'll have time to patch things up with a city magistrate he drinks with."

Longarm shrugged and said, "That's no big deal. I got me some vacation time coming. So maybe I'll drift down to Texas and look up some old pals."

"Marshal Vail says you're not to go anywhere near that loco cattle baroness with an all-points out on you, especially with the Texas Rangers knowing about you and that shameless bawd."

Longarm frowned and took a fistful of Henry's shirt gently but firmly in hand as he growled, "Let's get something straight, Henry. The lady of which you speak may ride astride and shoot pretty good for a female, but she's yet to do a thing she'd have call to feel ashamed of. So if you ever call her a bawd again, you're going to enjoy a life of eating soup unless you know a mighty fine dentist, hear?"

"Unhand me, you idiot!" Henry protested, adding, "I've been looking all over town for you to *help* you, not to get in a fistfight with you! People are starting to stare. Isn't there somewhere around here we could talk more privately?"

Longarm dragged Henry into a nearby beanery, shoved him down on a counter seat, and said, "Talk. I'm having eggs over chili con carne. The gal I was with last night meant well, I'm sure, but cold ham on rye just don't stick to a man's ribs after a hard night in the saddle."

As the pretty Mex waitress moved down the counter to take his order, Henry smoothed his shirtfront and got out a sheaf of yellow papers, saying, "Nothing for me, thanks. I'm a law clerk, not a fire-eater. As I was about to say before you were driven mad by hunger out front, Marshal Vail can't just say you wandered out of the office and that we can't rightly say when you might be back. You'll note these orders are predated as of yesterday. That's no doubt why you were so reluctant to hang about Police Head-quarters last night. You were already running a bit late when that MacTavish delayed you on your way to the Union Depot, right?"

"Sure," Longarm said. "I've been wondering why I had to get to the Union Depot so sudden. Where am I supposed to be going once I get there, Henry?"

Henry rolled his eyes heavenward and said, "Not *now,* damn it. The boss said to warn you the locals are sure to have the depot staked out. You're going to have to find some more discreet means of transportation and, by the way, your rooming house on the far side of Cherry Creek is staked out, too. So don't you dare go home for your saddle and Winchester."

"Damn it, Henry, I'm good at getting most anyplace I have to. But I like to know where that may *be,* before I start out."

The waitress slid Longarm's plate of eggs and chili con carne in front of him, along with a mug of black coffee and a slice of apple pie. As he dug right in, Henry shuddered and said, "It's easy to see how you've lived through so many gunfights. It's a waste of time, shooting a man with cast-iron innards. The mission we're sending you on winds you up in the cattle country of Utah. Catch a train out of anywhere but Denver and get off at Vernon. Do you know the place?"

Longarm scanned the mental map in his head a moment before he washed some eggs and chili down with coffee, nodded, and said, "I do. Ain't sure I'd call it cattle coun-try, though. Antelope and sheep do better on sagebrush than cows. So that's about all they have growing that far

21

out from the Mormon Delta. Who am I after, once I reach Vernon?"

"If we knew that we wouldn't have to send such a skilled deputy," Henry said. "We'd simply wire the local marshal and that would be that. Suffice it to say we've been picking up disturbing rumors about mysterious riders scaring the local Indians and homesteaders, both of whom are naturally under federal protection if and when the local sheriff can't, or won't, protect them."

Longarm swallowed a mouthful and asked, "How come the local sheriff won't protect 'em?"

"He denies anything at all unusual is going on. That's why Marshal Vail wants you to run over there and sort of sniff around. Somebody has to be a big fibber and you're pretty good at tripping fibbers up."

Henry could see Longarm's hunting instincts were already at work when he mused half to himself, "Hmm, it's ten to one the local sheriff's a Mormon, and you know how many nesters head west drinking coffee, smoking tobacco, and generally bending the Book of Mormon all out of shape. I could be wrong, though. Like I just said, Vernon lies out a ways from the Mormon Delta and nobody *raised* in them parts would be dumb enough to nest that far from all them irrigation works the saints spent so much time on."

"Saints?" asked Henry, and then, before Longarm could answer he nodded and said, "Right, Latter-Day Saints is what the Mormons call themselves. I don't recall typing up either term for you in those orders. As I told you, the whole affair is mighty mystic. Ah, don't you think you ought to get going, Longarm?"

The bigger and obviously hungrier federal employee said, "You go on back to the office if you've a mind to, old son." Then he called out, *"Señorita. Café mas, por favor."* So the waitress came over to refill his cup and bat her lashes at him, inspiring Henry to mutter, *"Merde alors,* if you want to show off," as he got up and left.

That left the field to Longarm. But while he could see the pretty little thing was breathing mighty passionate for so early in the morning, he knew he was asking for trouble if he hung about much longer. So he settled for just telling her he might be back to sample her hot tamales, and was about to overtip her and leave when he saw he'd already hung about too long. For old Sergeant Nolan of the Denver PD must have been feeling hungry, too. As the big burly Irishman settled next to him at the counter, Longarm said, "Morning, Nolan. I sure hope you just come in here for some chili con carne."

Nolan sort of growled, "Coffee was all I had in mind. I just put in a dreadful night, looking for you, Longarm."

The federal lawman sighed in resignation and asked, soberly, "What happens, now that you've found me?"

Nolan shrugged and replied, "Who says I found anybody? There are times a man has to go through the motions, when his captain is an asshole. That's not saying he'd be after collaring a man he owes his stripes to, would it?"

Longarm swallowed a lump of apple pie that seemed to be repeating on him before he said, flatly, "You don't owe me nothing. You earned them stripes fair and square, working on a case we just happened to be working together on."

Nolan chuckled and asked, "Are you sure your mother didn't come from Ireland, you big blarney-talking bullshitter? Don't try to tell a man you credited with cracking a case that was only confusing hell out of him whether he owes you or not. As I said, that captain is some sort of lunatic. But, sure and he's off duty by now, and none of the boys on the force who know you would be after bothering you."

"What about the ones who *don't* know me?" Longarm asked.

Nolan laughed and asked, "How could anyone who didn't know you arrest you? Where are you going from here? If you'll let me wake up with some Java I'll tag along and keep you out of trouble."

Longarm shook his head, rose from his stool, and said, "I don't want you to get in trouble, neither. If you were leaving town this morning, with the Denver PD looking for you, would you say the Union Depot was a good notion?"

"It's staked out," Nolan said. "But you'll pass through easy enough. The plainclothes lurking about the waiting room would be expecting the dreadful Longarm to be shorter, fatter, and clean-shaven, if you get my meaning."

"I'm not sure I do," Longarm said. "Who could have told them to watch for someone so ridiculous?" Then he nodded and said, "Oh, right. Thanks, old pard. Remind me to tell 'em you're a colored gent if ever *our* outfit is looking for *ybu*."

Nolan said that sounded fair, since he'd always been told his people were Black Irish. So they shook on it and parted friendly.

Up at the federal building, the pudgy Marshal Billy Vail was beaming at Henry as the clerk brought him up to date on his meeting with Longarm—well clear, thank God, of anywhere the police might expect to find him at this hour. Vail leaned back in this swivel chair, blowing cigar smoke that made Henry sort of wish for one of Longarm's notorious cheroots, and said, "Well, I ought to be able to calm the infernal city law down within a week at the most. It ain't like Longarm gunned a Denver minister, after all. MacTavish was wanted, federal. I'm just going to have to get that picky captain fired if he keeps frothing at the mouth about jurisdiction."

"Haven't you pointed out that a federal deputy on a mission has the right to bend the rules a bit, sir?"

Billy Vail was grinning wolfishly as he replied, "Why should I? The more he rants and raves the easier it will be to hang him once I get a certain city magistrate in the right mood. We'll just give Denver PD more rope, now that Longarm's safely on his way to nowheres much."

"I've been meaning to ask you about that, sir. Try as I might, I just can't see any reason to send a deputy with Longarm's seniority and skills so far, on the little we had to go on."

Vail blew a big stinky smoke ring before he smugly replied, "That's why you're the clerk and I run this office, my boy. Should you get caught in a serious fib, I'd have to fire you. But who's likely to fire *me*, as long as I don't lie to my superiors?"

Henry blinked and asked, "Are you saying I *lied* to Longarm in those orders I just handed him, sir?"

Vail shook his bullet head and said, "You didn't. *I* did. I'm allowed to because Longarm is my subordinate, not my superior, see?"

Then Vail noted the thundergasted expression on poor Henry's face and explained in a more fatherly tone, "Look, I would have sent him on a real mission if I'd had one to send him on. Was it my fault things have been so peaceful of late out our way?"

Henry gulped and said, "I guess not, sir. We had to get him out of town until this tempest with Denver PD blows over. But what on earth is poor Longarm supposed to do when he gets all the way to Utah and finds out nothing at all is going on?"

Vail shrugged and decided, "He'll think of something, if there happens to be a shapely ankle within miles. It'll serve him right if he don't. I picked a place as peaceful and far out of the way as I could come up with, knowing how much hell that boy can raise right here in Denver."

At the Union Depot, a friendly information clerk Longarm had done business with in the past was telling him that Vernon, Utah, was one of those places you couldn't get to from Denver, and that it still involved a heap of train transfers.

25

They settled on the whistle-stop at Lofgreen, a mite over ten miles from Vernon, and the clerk scribbled directions on the back of a timetable. As he handed it across the counter Longarm said he admired a railroader who could keep that much leaping on and off trains in his head. The railroader smiled modestly and told him, "I had to look it up the first couple of times. But you must be the tenth gent trying to get to Vernon in as many days."

As Longarm folded the instructions and put them away he tried to picture the out-of-the-way trail town he'd stopped for water in a time or two in the sagebrush and sheep country. Then he shook his head and decided, "There ain't ten good-looking gals in that bitty settlement. They must have had some other reason for going there. I don't suppose you recall what any of them old boys looked like?"

The railroader thought before he said, "Describe me a suspect and I likely told him how to get to Vernon, Longarm. They run from gents dressed more sedate than you to more than one I would have took for saddle tramps, if they'd been riding ponies instead of trains. I asked the seventh or eighth what everyone was headed to Vernon for. He told me to mind my own damned business. I figured I'd better. He wore his gun under his coat, cross-draw, like you. Didn't take him for a lawman, though."

"Was he dressed flashy enough for a tinhorn or broody enough to be a prosperous hired gun?" Longarm asked.

"I told you I felt it wiser not to inquire. His darker frock coat didn't need a pressing as bad yours does, if that's what you mean."

Longarm said that was close enough and went out on the platform to wait for the northbound. The platform was crowded. A lot of other folk knew the morning train to Cheyenne was due any minute. Most of them, cuss their hides, got to get *off* there. Longarm knew his own journey only began to head in a more sensible direction once he changed trains in Cheyenne.

26

Thanks to the unusual way he was headed out on this field mission, Longarm was packing no possibles. He was glad, once the Burlington combo pulled in and everyone tried to climb aboard at once, bashing one another with everything from carpetbags to Saratoga trunks. A sweet old lady tried to run Longarm through with her parasol. He was in enough trouble with Denver PD, so he let her win and made sure there were a couple of other passengers between them before he mounted the steps of the last coach. Once aboard, he turned left for the club car. He knew the reason everyone else was fighting to get aboard was that they never had enough seats on this run. Half the morning combo was freight cars, there were no Pullman cars, and what they offered in the way of coach seats were one-third plush and two-thirds hardwood. He knew he'd have enough of a time finding a place at the bar in the club car if he messed with searching for an infernal *seat*. So by the time the combo was rolling north Longarm was edged between one end of the bar and the grimy glass windows of the rear corner, sipping if not enjoying the first of the beers he'd consume between here and Cheyenne. It was a four or five hour trip, Lord willing, and if they didn't hit a cow. It was just as well the beer was flat and a mite warm. He had to pace himself for two good reasons. He hated to change trains on unsteady legs and, so far, he was on his own money and payday had been a spell back.

The travel orders he'd barely had time to scan had assured him the office would wire the six cents a mile and per diem expenses he was allowed in the field. Western Union could get most anywhere in the country in the time it took human beings and other real objects to get across town. But old Billy Vail could be sort of cheap, and there was no telling whether the money order waiting for him in Vernon would be enough, if things got complicated. Old Billy had grown up in the dear dead antebellum days when prices had been right, according to him. He just refused to believe a deputy in the field could spend as much as two bits a day for the hire of a mount, or fifty cents for a day's food and drink.

As the morning wore on, the sun kept rising and getting its back into heating up the already stuffy interior of the smoke-filled club car. So after he'd stood it a while Long-arm ordered a second beer and worked his way out to the observation platform.

Somebody cussed and slid the door shut after him. Longarm was more willing to accept a few cinders in his beer than some, if it meant he got to breathe. It was a lot cooler out on the bitty platform. Longarm knew he had it to himself this early because he'd been willing to surrender his place at the bar. He knew he'd play hell getting another drink between here and Cheyenne, but there were compensations. His hickory shirt already felt a lot drier under his stuffy coat. He took the coat off, along with his sweaty hat, and since there were no seats out on the platform, he hung them over a bulkhead lantern they only lit at night. Then, in shirtsleeves and vest, he braced his free hand on the brass railing and stood sipping sooty suds as the wind whipped through his hair and the tawny prairie on either side of the string-straight tracks receded at a fair clip.

He was less than halfway down his beer schooner when he heard the door slide open behind him and got a whiff of armpit and cigar smoke from inside. He'd hoped to enjoy the platform alone for at least a few more miles. But there was plenty of room and so he said, "Great minds run in the same channels," as he moved sideways and half turned to smile at some other sweaty soul.

The dapperly dressed newcomer was a sweaty soul who just might not have expected Longarm to move so grace-fully. For he had both hands out in front of him, aimed where Longarm's back had just been. So as Longarm grasped his intent, he let go his beer to grab the murderous stranger's sleeve, just behind the elbow, and speed him on his way. As the man who'd been about to push Longarm

28

over the railing wound up jackknifed over it himself, fighting for his balance, he gasped, "Have you gone crazy?" So Longarm said, "No, *you* have," and shifted his grip to the seat of the rascal's pants just long enough to boost him up and over, screaming like a schoolmarm who'd just seen a mouse.

He didn't scream long. A forward somersault off a train going forty miles an hour the other way would knock the wind out of many a schoolmarm, landing *right*. The unpleasant cuss wasn't that lucky. He landed on his head and then commenced to tumbleweed along the railroad ties for a couple of dozen bounces before he wound up a rapidly receding rag doll with its red stuffings knocked out.

Longarm casually drew his Colt and turned the other way as he heard the door slide open again. But it was old Gus, a Burlington conductor he knew of old. The older uniformed gent nodded when he saw it was Longarm and said, "Don't bother showing me your courtesy pass. I come to punch tickets when someone inside said there was at least two passengers out here."

"Who told you that?" Longarm asked. "I've a reason for asking."

Gus shrugged and said, "Barkeep, as a matter of fact. He must have been mistaken, right?"

"Wrong. I just tossed another gent off this train, pard."

The old-timer stared soberly at Longarm and said, "I'm sure you felt you had a good reason, Longarm. But would you mind telling me what it might have been? The front office asks such picky questions when someone finds a body along our right-of-way."

"I don't know if they'll find him dead on the tracks or not," Longarm said. "He might have had enough life left in him to crawl a ways, and you know how the coyotes are in these parts. But to answer your question, Gus, I threw him off because he seemed to be out to push *me* off."

Gus stared back along the receding tracks, not able to

make out much in the dust haze now, as he opined, "That sounds fair. But how come he was out to do you so dirty?"

Longarm shrugged and said, "Beats me. I never saw the cuss before I saw him coming at me fast and glare-eyed. What county are we in now, Gus?"

The old-timer glanced off to the west, spotted a telegraph pole he knew of old, and said, "I make it Weld County about now. Why do you ask?"

"I might wire the sheriff's department once we get to Cheyenne. There could be enough of him left for an educated guess as to who or what he might have been. A man in my line of work makes a lot of enemies. But I'm pretty good at remembering faces, and I'il be switched with snakes if I recall a time I might have done anything to make that face so mad at me. I don't think he was packing a gun. Nobody could be dumb enough to try what he just tried if he had some other way to kill a man. I think he just spotted me alone out here and acted out of sheer desperation."

Gus frowned and asked, "Desperation about what, Longarm? You just now said you didn't know the rascal. Couldn't he have waited until he could get to a gun, for Pete's sake?"

Longarm thought and decided, "He might not have known I didn't know him. I've had that happen to me a heap. Or he might have had some other reason for stopping me and just took the first chance he had."

Gus shook his head and said, "You mean he *thought* he had the chance. Nobody with a lick of sense would go after *you*, barehands, unless he was loco en la cabeza or, like you said, desperate."

"That's likely why they call some gents desperados," Longarm said. "I'm bound for Vernon, Utah, Gus. Would you know from your ticket punching if anyone else aboard this combo is on his way to the same parts?"

The old-timer blinked in surprise and replied, "Hell, no.

Why would anyone want to ride so far outta their way to get to that neck of the woods, Longarm? Didn't you know it was faster going over the Rockies from Denver aboard the D&RG Western?"

Longarm sighed fatalistically and said, "I might, *now.* Your man in Denver told me this was the easy way to get there. But, what the hell, we're halfways to Cheyenne and I know the way from there."

Gus spat over the rail and said, "Good help is sure hard to find these days. The other way would have saved you a couple of hours. But you're right. You may as well head for that mining area over the South Pass, now. You say you're looking for other gents getting there the hard way from Denver?"

Longarm got out a couple of cheroots and offered one to Gus as he replied, "They could be looking for me, seeing they all got the same bum steer. Vernon ain't the sort of place a lot of us would all be headed at once if something flashy wasn't going on there all of a sudden." He thumbed a match head alight and cupped it in his hands against the wind to light both their smokes as he continued, "I didn't have Vernon down as a mining town until you just now brung it up, Gus. Ain't it a mite south of that mining strip along the south shore of the Great Salt Lake?"

Gus got his own cheroot going before he said, "It is. A hard day's ride by horse. On the other hand, they've struck every color from copper to gold up around Bingham Canyon, and I just can't see such a sudden stampede after sagebrush and sheep, can you?"

Longarm glanced south along the receding tracks as he shook his head and said, "I don't suspect that rascal who just tried to kill me was a sheepherder. He looked more like the sort of tinhorn boomer you run across in a gold rush."

Then a couple more overheated passengers came out on the platform and he told Gus it had been nice talking to

31

him. As the old-timer went back inside with his ticket punch, Longarm put his hat and coat back on to follow. He was dried cool. The interior had aired out some, and if anyone else was out to push him off the damned train Longarm meant to make them work at it.

Chapter 3

There was a Western Union office attached to the depot when Longarm got off at Cheyenne. So he checked his timetable, saw he could just about make it, and went to wire the sheriff's department of Weld County about the mysterious stranger he'd left to their jurisdiction. He thought about wiring Billy Vail the same news, but decided it could wait until he knew something.

As he moved back toward the loading platforms through the cavernous smoke-filled waiting room, he almost passed a small familiar figure seated on one of the benches. It was that sassy little whore-orphan he thought he'd straightened out the night before. As he stopped to stare soberly down at her, she stared back up at him, defiantly, and asked, "Have you been following me, you dirty old man?"

Longarm sighed and told her, "I was about to ask you the same thing, you dirty little gal. I thought we'd agreed that running off from that orphan asylum before you matured a mite sounded sort of dumb."

33

She shrugged and said, "You was the one doing all the preaching. I learned a long time ago not to argue with my elders, direct."

He nodded and said, "I might have known. You just pretended to go back to bed and then, as soon as nobody was standing right over you, you lit out. Did you steal a horse, like I asked you not to?"

She shook her head and said, "It wasn't too far to walk and, like I told you, the night was still young and *some* men find me prettier than *you* seem to. Of course, not many of the cowhands along Larimer ever get a crack at anything as tempting as Miss Morgana. The two of you sure was making a lot of noise as I crept past her door on my way out."

Longarm scowled down at her and said, "Blackmail is more disgusting than your usual line of work. So listen sharp and I'll tell you why that ain't the reason I'm not dragging you right back to Denver with a well-tanned rump."

She seemed to be paying attention as he told her, "Whoring ain't a federal offense. Neither is running away from your lawful guardian. I could turn you in to the local law. But since you've made it across a state line, getting you back to Denver would be a chore, and you'd no doubt run away again in less time than it would take Miss Morgana to have you extradited. So we wouldn't be doing her a favor even if she wanted a brat like you molesting her more innocent orphans."

"What are you going to do then?" she asked. "I'll go along with most anything that ain't actually painful."

He chuckled despite himself and said, "I'm not going to do a thing. I got a train to catch and there's a limit to how many times I'm supposed to set even you on the straight and narrow."

She stuck out her lower lip and protested, "You was screwing Miss Morgana, wasn't you?"

"Whether I was or wasn't, she's a grown woman,

though I doubt she's had as much experience with men as you, despite your tender years. I can see now it was a mistake to save you from the alley thug you were working with a spell back. You ain't no abused child. You're a child who abuses everyone who tries to help you, and any gal who can slicker *me* can doubtless handle most of the men she's apt to meet up with along the primrose path."

"Then you're going to let me go?" she asked, hopefully.

He shrugged and said, "I'd say you were long gone before I ever met you. Since you refuse to act like the child you are, let's just hope you don't wind up clapped or beaten to death by the time you reach the lawful age of consent. I doubt you will. But, like I said, I can't save the whole world, and there's a heap of halfway decent kids worth saving. So *via con Dios,* you little sass, and should anyone ever ask, I don't remember running into you today."

He ticked the brim of his Stetson to her and continued on his way. He knew better than to look back. But when he got to the platform archway he did, to see her sitting there like a lost pathetic child, which she was, in truth. Then he forced himself to turn his back on her again. It made him feel bad. But that was the way life was. There were kids going hungry all over the world right now. He knew she could take care of herself better than a lot of kids her age. He couldn't do anything about any of them. So he went out to wait for the UP Westbound.

It pulled in before he could be tempted to go back and make another futile attempt to reform the wayward little tramp. There were more seats on the cross-country flier. More than one was occupied by a lady who seemed to be traveling alone. But Longarm was feeling a mite disgusted with horny men who just couldn't behave themselves with women, or vice versa. He might not have felt so inspired to purity if he was going on all the way to the west coast with any gal who might want to join him for some soda pop, or if he'd had a mite more money to spend on the same. But

35

until he picked up that money order in Vernon he figured he'd best heed his own words on the wages of sin.

It was just as well he resisted the temptation of a mighty pretty but mighty expensive looking gal in the last coach. For when he got back to the club car he found a poker game in progress and, after he'd watched from the bar a spell, decided to sit in. Card playing could be more expensive and a lot less fun than picking up strange women on a train, provided the game was being played on the level. But this one wasn't and, while Longarm never cheated at cards against honest men, he thought it only fair to fleece a fleecer, and the mechanic in the checked suit with his back to the window was dealing so raw and dirty it was a wonder to Longarm he was still alive.

He waited until a mousy little gent in a snuff-colored suit announced the stakes were getting too rich for his blood and got up to leave a folding chair vacant. Nobody seemed to object when Longarm sat down and pulled it closer to the bitty table bolted to the deck. The gent in the checked suit introduced himself as a traveling salesman called Linkletter and announced the ante was two bits. He tried to assure the newcomer further by dealing a fair first hand. Longarm let it show on his face. He knew the card shark knew what he was holding, and it never paid to let a man know you had a poker face before it was time to play poker.

The shark didn't let Longarm win the first modest pot. That might have seemed obvious, even to the sort of fools who played cards with strangers on a train. The mining man seated to Longarm's left raked in the pile of quarters, beating Longarm by only one wild card, lest he feel *too* discouraged.

The next pot, bigger by a good ten bucks, went to the rancher seated to Longarm's right. Then it was Longarm's turn to win and, as the card shark had hoped, Longarm grinned like a country boy and raised the ante to four bits.

He acted like a sport when the mining man won the next

more serious pot. It was hard to believe that neither he nor the rancher found it odd that Linkletter seemed so cheerful about his own dismal luck, or that having started the game as dealer he didn't seem to want anyone else dealing, as custom decreed. Longarm could tell from the way the mining man and rancher held their cards and read them that neither was in the custom of playing poker for real money.

By this time Longarm had had time to examine his own cards pretty good and, as he'd suspected from the bar, found none of them had been marked. A slicker who hogged the dealing didn't need to play with a marked deck when he wore a big silver ring with a mirror finish. The deck was new but the same cheap brand sold in many a drinking establishment on demand. So Longarm was as surprised as Linkletter likely was when the mining man took umbrage at losing three times in a row and asked in a polite but firm voice if they could have a fresh deck.

Linkletter never let on if he felt insulted. He just called out to the barkeep right behind Longarm and the car attendant brought a sealed fresh deck over, pocketed the tip, and paid the barkeep. Linkletter cranked the window behind him open to toss the old cards out, saying, dryly, "It's less confusing when we know where all the aces might be."

Then, as everyone else chuckled, the tension broken, Linkletter broke open the fresh deck, shuffled, and almost as an afterthought asked Longarm if he wanted to deal. Longarm shook his head and said, "You go ahead. You've been doing fine so far, and I confess I'm all thumbs."

The card shark didn't ask if anyone else wanted to deal, since he'd satisfied one and all by offering to a man he could see was a mite clumsy-handed. He shuffled again and dealt Longarm the winning hand this time. The pot had now grown to a handsome pile of quarters. Longarm was tempted to quit while he was ahead. But how often did a man get such a crack at a high-rolling card shark? He decided it was time to raise the ante to a dollar.

Across the table, Linkletter looked as if he was about to

come over and kiss Longarm, although he did his best to hide it. Longarm knew he was playing right into the card shark's hands, or so the card shark thought. All three of his suckers were about even, and Linkletter knew that when it was time to make the kill he'd be able to point out it hadn't been *his* notion to raise the stakes so high. The question in Longarm's mind was simply how big a pot Linkletter was figuring on before he stole it. He'd seen this drama played out before, sometimes with noisy results. The mining man was getting hard-eyed as the game got more serious, and the rancher was packing a Smith and Wesson .44 on his hip. Longarm doubted the so-called salesman would push his luck to more than a hundred from each sucker. The mining man looked like he'd be a sore loser at a hundred, in fact.

So Longarm watched and waited until, sure enough, Linkletter had dealt him a pretty good hand and then raised, with a sort of hesitant expression on his face. Longarm could tell the other two suckers were holding high cards, too, when they proceeded to toss coin after coin into the pot. Longarm had to do the same thing, of course. The mining man looked as if he was about to drop out. But Linkletter must have dealt him something awesome. For he stayed in as the pot got sweeter and then it was Longarm's turn. So he gulped and asked, "Is it my understanding we're still playing deuces wild?"

Linkletter, who knew damned well Longarm was holding only one wild card, nodded expansively. So Longarm raised. The rancher shook his head sadly and said, "My old woman will skin me alive if I lose more than that."

Linkletter raised again. The mining man shook his head and folded. That left Longarm and the card shark, with close to four hundred on the table between them. Linkletter must have figured that was enough. He said, "I knew my luck would change if I hung in long enough," and spread his flush on the table for the world to admire. But as he moved to take in his winnings, Longarm spread his own hand, saying, "Not so fast, pard. With four deuces I make this a full house or better."

There was a stunned silence as Longarm placed his hat upside down in his lap and proceeded to scoop it full of quarters. He knew the card shark knew what he'd done. But as he'd assumed, the professional would have taken up bank robbing by this time if he was willing to risk gunplay for money. As Longarm rose with the hatful of heavy silver the mining man growled, "Sit down. The game ain't over yet."

"It is for me," Longarm said. "I got to get off long before I can ever hope to be dealt a hand like that again."

As the mining man half rose, Longarm placed the hat on the nearby bar, let his coat fall open to expose his gun grips, and added in a less friendly voice, "Don't." And then, as the mining man decided it wasn't worth it, Longarm asked the barkeep if he could use some change. He kept his eyes on the three men at the nearby table as the barkeep changed his winnings to silver certificates and a handful of silver dollars, asking, "Do you want to count it, Longarm?"

The tall deputy said he was sure he could trust a gent who knew him and, as the name sank in, the surly mining man's face went frog-belly white. Linkletter laughed almost boyishly and said, "I might have known. The least you can do is buy us a round of drinks, you innocent-looking greenhorn."

They all laughed, the tension broken. As they bellied up to the bar, Linkletter waited until his other two suckers got to talking about something else before he quietly asked Longarm, "How did you do that?" Then, when Longarm innocently asked what he was talking about, the card shark said, "Let me guess. You bought your own deck from behind this very bar before you buzzed so blindly into my web. What tipped you off?"

Longarm sipped some suds before he said, "Well, seeing as you took it so gracefully, I may as well allow that

39

mirrored ring you're sporting tipped me off to your plan of action. Had you displayed less taste in jewelry I'd have figured marked cards, and that would have been a lot tougher."

"Would you have tried to take me, anyway?" the card shark asked.

Longarm answered, truthfully, "Not as a rule. I'm a lawman, not a gambling man. But at the moment I'm on a serious mission without much dinero in my pockets. Or, that is, I *was* until I saw what was up and sort of took advantage of you. I hope you're not sore. I'll be getting off at Ogden and you'll have all the way to Frisco to recoup your modest losses."

Linkletter grimaced and said, "You mean Reno. I'm headed for a silver strike where it may be safer to play for real money."

Longarm said that sounded fair and added, "Are you sure you're going that far, pard? I heard something's up just south of the Great Salt Lake and that's mining country too, you know."

The card shark shook his head and said, "You're talking about established low-grade mining, not bonanza. I've tried the bitty mining camps in them parts, Longarm. There's some gold and more silver. But it's mostly copper, and it's all dug by hard-rock hands on modest day wages. You only get big spenders around new strikes. The boys working between the lake and Bingham Canyon take their money right home to the little women. Nobody but the big mining companies get rich on low-grade mining, and they just don't allow the likes of me in their private clubs back east."

Longarm sipped some more beer as he thought about that. Then he said, "I reckon a traveling tinhorn like you, no offense, would hear about sudden pay dirt before the rest of us would. So, taking you at your own word, something mighty odd is going on south of that low-grade mining area we all admire. Are you sure you've heard nothing about sudden wealth in or about the desert town of Vernon?"

Linkletter shook his head and said, "Never heard of the place. What rail line is it on?"

"It ain't," Longarm said. "I got to get off ten or more miles away and hire a mount. The last time I looked, Vernon was a wide spot in a sheep trail, catering to the needs of stockmen and Mormons who don't drink enough to keep a decent saloon going. Yet I know for a fact that something's up down yonder and that at least a dozen or so other gents with guns have recently been headed the same place. It sure makes one wonder what the hell all them sheep could be up to, all of a sudden."

Chapter 4

What with one thing and another, including a gal in Ogden who seemed willing to help him pass the time until another train came in, Longarm got to the whistle-stop of Lofgreen just about sundown. That wasn't where he was supposed to be, of course. So he worked out a deal with the one and only livery in town for a fair stock saddle and a walleyed buckskin mare they'd doubtless meant to sell for glue before Longarm showed up just in time to save her.

She failed to show much gratitude as he rode her out of town in the gathering dusk. The trail to Vernon was easy enough to see, but for some reason she kept wandering off through the stirrup-high sage. It was a pain in the ass to ride a bronc you had to steer all the way like a rickety old bicycle. He told her, "It's a good thing we ain't going far, you bat-blind jug-head. For if Vernon was far enough for me to consider night camp, guess who I'd have for supper?"

The flat range cooled sudden after sundown, and the full

moon rising to the east made it tempting to lope most of the ten or so miles ahead. But when Longarm tried to get her to go, the old buckskin just stopped and craned her head around to stare back at him sadly with her one good eye. He said, "I don't know how to tell you this. But it's generally held that when a rider heels a mount's ribs he expects her to move faster, not stop."

She finally moved on in a half-baked, uncomfortable trot. He let it go at that, and just under two hours later they got to Vernon. He reined in at the Western Union office across the street from the town lockup, and the old mare had her muzzle down in a watering trough, gulping fit to bust, before he could dismount. He tied the reins to the hitching rail on the far side of the trough—in the unlikely event the buckskin had enough ambition to move without having her ribs pounded—and strode on into the telegraph office, muttering about all females in general.

The wispy-haired old clerk on night duty inside said they sure enough had connections to Denver, but that, no, there was no such thing as a message, let alone a money order, for anyone named Long. The puzzled Longarm muttered, "That's mighty damned inconsiderate, even for old Billy Vail. He had to know I was on my way here short of money, for he sent me here after paying me himself, over two weeks ago."

Then he tore a telegram blank from the pad on the counter and penciled a terse message to the home office, informing Vail he was here in Vernon and, damn it, broke. What he won at poker on his own was none of Billy Vail's business, and it said right in the Constitution of these United States that nobody had to work for nothing, no more, even for the Justice Department.

He handed the form over and asked the clerk to send it night letter rates, collect. The clerk pointed out that as long as he was sending it night letter rates he had a lot more words coming to him, free. But Longarm said, "I said all I have to say. Your company would only cross out the words

43

if I put down what I think of the thoughtless bastard in plain English. Just see that my office gets my message, come morning, and maybe the old fart will recall sending me all the way out here without a dime in traveling expenses. I'll check back with you all before noon."

Then, having reported in to Vail, Longarm headed across the way to pay the usual courtesy call on the local law.

This turned out to be an old desert rat with a brass badge and tobacco-stained beard. He told Longarm it was all right to call him Pop, since everyone else did, and added that he'd just been fixing to close up for the night. He jerked a horny thumb over his shoulder at the empty patent cell behind his desk as he explained business was usually slow at this time of the year.

Longarm said, "Far be it from me to keep you up past your bedtime, Pop. But weren't you one of the gents who asked my outfit for help out here?"

The old man stared blankly up at Longarm and seemed sincere as he denied it, asking, "What in thunder would I be sending for a federal deputy for, Longarm? It's high summer between roundups and most of the really tough Basques in these parts are out on the range screwing sheep. There ain't two hundred white folk who live in this town regular, and they all gets along tolerable."

"That's not the way my travel orders read," Longarm said. "I'll allow they don't go into much detail, even reading them more than once aboard the train. But according to my boss, Marshal Vail, we were asked to investigate reports of mysterious strangers scaring Indians and abusing settlers, or maybe it's the other way around. I've seldom been sent out on the field with such vague orders. Are you sure nobody's complained to you about night riding Danites, Pop? No offense, but I can see you chew more tobacco than the saints approve of, and they hardly tell us gentile lawmen about such matters."

The old-timer shrugged and said, "The Avenging

44

Angels, or Danites, as you and the brethren call 'em, haven't been raising all that much hell since the army hung Brother Lee. The Salt Lake temple's been trying to convince Washington that Utah ought to be a state, and to do so they've cut out a lot of their early odd ways. Mormons and gentiles get along all right, around here. They don't mind my being town marshal and I don't worry about a couple of old-timers who have more wives than any man with a lick of sense would know what to do with. It sounds to me you've been sent on a wild-goose chase, son. I know most of the settlers within a good day's ride and nobody's been pestering 'em."

"What about the Indians?" Longarm asked.

"There ain't none, close enough to matter. Nearest reserve is Skull Valley, twenty miles or more from here. We get some of the agency folk in here now and again, shopping. Ain't heard a word about anyone pestering any pesky redskins though. It's usually the other way around. But I don't recall anyone losing a pony to a Pauite since we hung the last one, two or three summers back."

Longarm tried, "Let's just talk about strangers in general, then. I know for a fact that some other gents were asking a railroad man in Denver how to get here ahead of me."

The old-timer rose, stretched, and said, "I got to close up and get on home, son. There's strangers coming through here all the time. That's how come they call this a trail town. We're on the north–south trail between the Great Salt Lake and the Sevier River to the south. Folk ride through here going one place or the other. I don't recall anyone mysterious *staying* here in Vernon, ever. Like I said, it's a quiet little town where everybody knows everyone else. I'd have surely heard about it if anyone was having trouble. You can hear a man beating his wife from one end of town to the other."

Since the town law was sort of herding him out the door, Longarm had no way, short of rudeness, to prolong the dumb conversation. So they shook on it friendly out front, and Longarm headed for the only saloon he recalled in town to see if he could at least find something to eat and a place to stay until such time as Billy Vail sent more details, or at least some money.

The nameless little taproom, catering only to the gentile minority in town or passing through, made the dinky Longbranch in Dodge look like a palace. It was set in a storefront not much wider than the average locksmith shop. The bar running back one side took up most of the room. There wasn't floor space for any tables or chairs. When Longarm asked the sleepy cuss behind the fake mahogany if they served room and board as well as rotgut, the barkeep told him not to talk silly and added, "You might try the Wilson widows on the edge of town, where the trail fords the creek. They mostly raise poultry. But they've been known to put a passing-through rider up for a few nights."

Longarm allowed he was obliged for the information and asked about livery service for his buckskin. The barkeep told him that if the Wilson widows took him in they'd have a place for his pony. If they were full up, they wouldn't, and nobody else in town had room, board, or stable for hire. Longarm figured the least he owed the informative barkeep was the purchase of a beer. But the easy-going local told him, "You don't have time. Folk turn in with the chickens in these parts, and the widows won't open their door to no stranger once they're in their nightgowns."

Longarm settled for offering the barkeep a smoke and even lighting it for him as he observed, "I notice you call the ladies widows, in the plural sense."

"The two of them was married up with the same saint, Hank Wilson," the barkeep explained. "He got thrown and stomped by a mustang he was trying to break about two years ago come roundup. He was a tough old boy. A man married up to two gals at once would have to be. But that

46

wild stud he was trying to tame must have been even more exciting to mess with."

Longarm lit his own smoke and ambled out to see if he could find the poultry spread the barkeep had suggested. The one main street lay silver-dusted and deserted by the light of the overhead moon. He saw someone had tethered another mount next to his buckskin across the way. It was a black pony with a silver-mounted, center-fire saddle. Its owner was likely in the Western Union on his own business at this hour.

Longarm learned how wrong he'd just guessed when a voice behind him growled, "Freeze!"

Longarm did so, since he didn't seem to have much choice in the matter, but he couldn't help saying, "You got the drop on me. But after that it just gets silly, pard. I'm a lawman, not a suspicious vagrant."

The man covering him from the rear replied, "I know who you are, Longarm. Now I want you to reach under that frock coat with your left hand, slow, and then I want you to unbuckle your gun rig and let it fall, quiet, to the dust."

Longarm shrugged and proceeded to do that, as well, asking if the mysterious stranger would like to tell him what this was all about. The other man waited until Longarm's .44-40 was on the ground and out of Longarm's possible reach before he said, in a more jovial tone, "Just start walking and, like the old song says, farther along we'll know more about it."

Longarm stepped over his gun belt but only moved a few paces before he asked just where the other man wanted him to head for.

The stranger Longarm had yet to see said, "Either direction right or left will do as well, since we're about in the center of a mighty small town right now."

Longarm turned left, saying, "They told me you can hear a man beating his wife from one end of town to the other. I take it we have some business to discuss more private, out among the silvery sage bushes?"

The man with the drop on him said, "They told me you was smart. Maybe too smart for your own good. Just keep walking and let's not consider nothing tricky. I don't want to gun you within the city limits. But if I have to, I can likely ride out before anyone gets around to asking pesky questions, see?"

Longarm could see all too well. But he kept walking as he said, "I can see you're holding the winning hand this evening. But as long as I seem so doomed, would you mind telling me who sent you after me?"

The man marching him toward the privacy of the open range told him, "It's a long story and it ain't as if you'll get to *remember* any of it. Let's just say you should have stayed in Denver. I got nothing personal against you, my ownself. But the gent I works for says lawmen like you ought to be stomped out, lest they multiply."

Longarm shrugged and kept walking. He'd noticed, riding in, that Vernon was a small town. But somehow it looked as if it had shrunk even more since then. For they passed the last houses to the south even sooner than he'd wanted to. Longarm knew the sound of gunshots carried well over a mile, but didn't draw much attention, even at night, from a quarter mile away. He told the hired gun behind him, "I wish I could talk you out of this grim notion. But if I can't, how much farther do you aim to march me?"

"Oh, I reckon this is about far enough."

Longarm turned around, with a resigned smile, and as soon as he was facing the son of a bitch, let him have both barrels of his derringer.

Longarm's vest-pocket gun made a heap of noise for its size, since he loaded it with serious rounds in case events like this one arose. But in his haste he'd only managed to shoot his target low, but not instantly fatal. So as he retraced his steps to kick the other man's six-gun into the brush, the man he'd put on the ground was able to moan, "Who shot me, damn it?"

Longarm hunkered down beside him to see what his two derringer slugs had wrought as he explained, pleasantly, "I'm sorry I gut-shot you. But it was your own fault, making me palm my belly gun left-handed. I'd have nailed you clean at that range if I'd been shooting right-handed. But don't cry too much. It won't hurt you in a few minutes."

They could both hear dogs barking and doors popping open in the near distance. Longarm saw at least two of the townsmen on their way to investigate the gunplay were packing lanterns. But he still struck a match for a better look at the dying gunslick's face while it could still talk to him.

As the flickering flame illuminated the clean-shaven, petulant features of the man he'd turned the tables on, Longarm whistled and said, "Well, howdy, Handsome Luke. I'd heard you escaped from Yuma Prison. I frankly figured you'd lay low a spell before you advertised your gun for hire again."

The well-known but hardly admired gunslick muttered a terrible thing about Longarm's mother. Longarm chuckled fondly, split a pouty lip with an almost gentle backhanded blow, and said, "We don't have time to swap insults, old son. You're fixing to die, either way. I might let you die in more comfort if you saw fit to tell me who you were working for."

The shot-up killer moaned, "You ain't allowed to torture me, you cruel bastard."

Longarm hit him again and growled, "Feel free to *sue* me when you're up and about again. Who sent you? I don't want to grab you by the balls any more than you might want me to. But you ain't about to go gentle into the great beyond before you tell me what I need to know."

Handsome Luke proved Longarm wrong. He never so much as gave a gasp when Longarm grabbed him by the

49

crotch, hard. So Longarm let go, seeing as the son of a bitch had up and died on him so sissy.

Longarm fumbled a couple of loose rounds from a coat pocket, reloaded the derringer, and snapped it back to his watch chain. Then he rose to search for the more serious gun he'd kicked off the trail. He'd just found it with a boot tip and picked it up by the time the crowd from town arrived to shed more light on the subject. He spotted old Pop's brass badge glinting in the lantern light and walked over to him, saying, "Lucky for me the gent you see on the ground was holding this double-action Lightning .38 on me. A cocked '74 thumb buster can go off inconvenient as hell."

Pop held his lantern right above the remains of Handsome Luke as he answered, "Anyone can see what an awful mistake this old boy just made, Longarm. But who in thunder is he, or was he?"

Longarm could see better, as well. After putting two rounds in what had been little more than a black blur he found it mildly surprising to gaze down at such a fancy black and silver charro outfit. The two places he'd hit the rascal blossomed shiny wet crimson in the coal-oil light. Longarm figured the puncture just above the fancy belt had occasioned most of the groaning, while the round just under the heart accounted for the shortness of the conversation. He told Pop, "His handle was Handsome Luke Harding. Hired gun. He was supposed to be doing life at Yuma as the result of a clumsy shoot-out and a mighty fine lawyer. As you can see, he wasn't in Yuma this evening. I wasn't able to find out who sent him after me, but he did admit he'd been sent. I sure wish someone could tell me which direction he rode in from, at least."

Six or eight members of the crowd allowed they'd never laid an eye on the fancy-dressed rascal before. Then an older gent dressed sober enough to be a Mormon elder, praise the Lord, cleared his throat and opined, "I think I saw him earlier, riding down from the north as I was rocking on my front porch after supper, an hour or so back. I recall remarking on those silver conchas down his pants leg as they winked at me in the moonlight. He was mounted show-off gentile, too. How many serious stockmen work out of a silver-mounted saddle?"

Longarm blessed the elder and told Pop, "That works better than if he was following me, seeing as I came most of the way here by train. Someone knew I was coming and sent him to head me off. I didn't know I was coming, until mighty recent, so someone else must have wired ahead."

"I don't see how anyone could have Western Unioned him here, Longarm," Pop said. "You just showed up, and he wasn't in town at all until even later."

"That's what I just said," Longarm replied. "We're talking about another town, no more than a day's ride from here, with telegraph facilities. Your move."

Pop shrugged and said, "Hell, the wires follow the trail and the trail runs from the south shore of the Great Salt Lake to the irrigated spreads down south."

Just then a teenager in bib overalls joined the group around the body, holding Longarm's holstered .44-40 like a sandwich with the unbuckled belt flapping against his right leg. He said he'd just found it in the street near the saloon, and asked if it might belong to anyone out this way. Longarm claimed it with a nod of thanks and proceeded to strap it back on under his coat as he went on with Pop, "This rascal wasn't sent north from the farms along the river. That halves it to somewhere between here and the mining country to the north. Handsome Luke would have had a time passing himself off as a Paiute. So that eliminates the reservation telegraph office at Skull Valley. How many places does that give us within forty miles, tops?"

Pop shifted his cud, spat, and said, "Bingham Canyon's less'n fifty miles. There's maybe a dozen trail stops between here and there, though none so grand as Vernon. You know how ambitious merchants will set up shop at ever' cross-trail or water hole along a well-traveled trail. Most general stores double as post offices and telegraph outlets, given half the chance. But we're talking bitty country hamlets, Longarm. I can't think of no place such a flashy stranger could have spent much time in unnoticed."

Longarm adjusted the weight on his left hip until his six-gun felt more comfortable while he said, "A notorious gunslick on the dodge wouldn't have been holed up in any small town. He'd have been staying with closer friends at some spread, sending or more likely getting wires from other parts by using a more innocent looking rider as a go-between. I mean to ask questions as I work my way north, but I'd know what to ask, better, if I had any idea what the rascals are worried about my finding out." He turned to the crowd in general to ask, "Have any of you gents heard talk of anyone, red or white, being threatened, or even suspicious of any other recent strangers?"

There was a low rumble of negative helpfulness. Longarm sighed and said, "That's what I was afraid of. I was sent here in answer to such complaints. I know some other outsiders have passed this way recently in suspicious numbers. But since none of you are complaining and none of them other gents have lingered here in Vernon, I have to be in the wrong place."

"I told you that earlier," Pop said. "The only trouble we've had in Vernon for years is spread out at our feet right now, and he wasn't after any of *us*. I know you only done what you had to, Longarm. We'd still best go back into town and wire the more serious county law about what happened here, just now."

Everyone else murmured agreement. Pop said, "Let's go. I'll send a buckboard out for this dead cuss. The county will no doubt want us to salt him down and get him up to the county seat, closer to the lake."

Longarm fell in step with Pop and the others, lest he be left out here alone in the dark again. But as they moved back toward the city lights, he told the older lawman, "It's a shame my boss frowns on federal deputies putting in for

52

bounty money. Handsome Luke sure had a lot of paper out on him."

Pop moved on a few paces and another spit before, as Longarm had hoped he might, he asked in a desperately casual voice how much money they were discussing. When Longarm opined it had to run close to four figures, the old-timer spat again and observed, "Just my luck they sent him after you instead of me. You'd think a wanted man, out to gun lawmen, would show more consideration. *I* got no reservations about putting in for bounty money, you know."

Longarm never would have brought it up if he hadn't known. But he'd learned not to sound too eager to get out of the paperwork. He let the older lawman chew on the notion for a dozen more paces before he said, absently, "It does seem a shame that your county sheriff figures to wind up with the bounty on the son of a bitch, after *we* done all the work down this way."

Pop shot him a stricken look and demanded to know how in the name of all that's good and fair Tooele County rated the reward for Handsome Luke's demise. So Longarm explained, *"Somebody* is sure to put in for it, once they see the fliers reading dead or alive. I ain't allowed to, but hell, *somebody* has to get it, right?"

Pop protested, "That well may be, old son. But the son of a bitch was killed in *my* jurisdiction, not that damned old sheriff's."

"Yes and no," Longarm said. "This is your township, but since we happen to be in Tooele County—"

"Hold on, damn it," Pop cut in, chewing faster and no doubt thinking even harder as he almost pleaded, "What if we was to say you was working with me against a suspicious character I sort of spotted first? If I was to word my report just right, I might be able to collect that bounty money and split it with you, sort of unofficial, see?"

Longarm had hoped the old-timer was that smart. But he said, "I dunno, Pop. If my boss saw my name anywhere in connection with the sudden end of Handsome Luke's career he'd grill hell out of me. Old Billy's a suspicious cuss and I'd be sore-put to spend even my own money freely for a spell. But what if you was to put down a sort of freestyle shooting between you and *your* deputies and a wanted man who decided to make a fight of it when *you* told him he was under arrest?"

Pop had to spit twice on that notion. Then he said, "Well, it could be took that way, when you consider harder. I don't have no regular deputies. But I surely *would* have told the cuss he was under arrest if I'd seen him under my jurisdiction in a more upright condition."

Longarm said, "There you go, Pop. Nobody's likely to ask anyone else in town any picky details and, hell, they're your friends, ain't they?"

Pop brightened and said, "Sure they are and, better yet, none of 'em seen the way me and you shot it out with that dead outlaw. I can see just how I ought to report it to the county, terse. My wires to the folk kind enough to post good money on the rascal's dead hide can read even terser. But about your cut, pard . . ."

"I'd best just settle for a favor or two my boss won't be able to put numbers to," Longarm said. "I got this far aboard a piss-poor livery nag. With your permission, I mean to ride on, come sunrise, aboard that fine black pony Handsome Luke has no possible further use for. I'd like you all to return the buckskin to Lofgreen for me when you've the time and someone riding that way."

Pop said they had a deal on that, but added, "Has it occurred to you that black pony and fancy saddle might be easy for friends of the man you just killed to recognize, old son?"

"I'm sort of counting on it. If that hired gun has been hiding out on some local spread, the pony they let him beg, buy, or borrow might just know the way home, as well."

Chapter 5

The barkeep who'd told Longarm about the Wilson widows had been right about folk turning in early in these parts. Longarm saw no lights lit in the frame house as he tethered the black pony to the picket fence out front. But while he'd found a .44-40 Winchester lashed to the swells of his fine new saddle, the late Handsome Luke, like himself, had been traveling light, with no bedroll or even water bags. So spending the rest of the night under the stars amid the silvery sage promised to freeze his ass more than he wanted it frozen. For summer or winter, the Great Basin's thin, dry air got cold as a banker's heart by around midnight.

He mounted the plank steps to search for a knocker or doorbell in the deep shadows of the porch. Then he spied a ghostly glow through the lace curtains, and a sort of ghostly form seemed to be wafting toward him down the hallway inside. When she opened the door he could see she looked more solid, standing there in her white cotton nightgown with her blond hair down and a candle in one hand. She said she wasn't buying any and that this was a hell of a time to peddle brushes to a poor old widow woman in any case.

He figured she was closer to a well-preserved thirty than old. But he told her she couldn't be more than sixteen and added that he'd been told she and her, ah, co-wife were said to offer room and board to wayfaring strangers, such as himself.

She held her candle higher for a better look at him. Then she must have decided she liked what she saw. For she smiled and told him, "You're too late for a warm supper, the fire's long gone to its rest for the night. We could fix you up with cold cuts and sort of warm lemonade. But we're saints, so you can't have coffee, tea, or any other sinful liquids. We don't allow smoking under our roof, neither. If that hasn't scared you off, our rates are a dollar a day."

Longarm didn't point out that it was night. He asked if that included his pony and she said, "If you tend him yourself. Lead him around to the stable out back and cross the yard to our kitchen door when you're done. You'll find hay and cracked corn above the stalls. The buckets and water pump are by the door. I'll see what we can whip up for you in the kitchen in the meantime. Could I have that dollar now?"

He smiled and reached in his pocket for a cartwheel. She took it with a less suspicious smile and shut the door in his face.

He chuckled, went back to the road, and told the black pony things were looking up as he led it through the gate and around the house. As they crossed the moonlit yard a mess of chickens and at least one goose, if it wasn't a hissing serpent, gave 'em hell. But he saw all the poultry had been cooped secure for the night. In coyote country even geese had to spend the nights behind locked doors.

The stable smelled clean, for a stable, and as he lit a

handy lamp to chore his own mount he saw the two other ponies stalled for the night had been currycombed recently. He led the black pony into a vacant stall, removed the fancy saddle and bridle, and draped them over the side of the stall. When he spotted the ferocious Spanish bit the late Handsome Luke had been riding with he whistled softly, patted the pony's neck, and told it, "I can see why you've been so responsive to neck reining, up to now. I fear we won't have time to fit you with a more civilized bit, old pard. But I'll remember to treat you gentle if you'll re- member I seldom aims a mount gee or haw unless I mean it."

He filled the built-in trough with water, poured a couple of quarts of cracked corn in the feed box, and skipped the hay. It smelled fresh-cured, but summer-dried grass came free on the open range and there was no telling when he'd get a chance to feed the critter right again.

As the black pony buried its tender muzzle in the water without even sniffing at the feed box, Longarm nodded and said, "I figured you'd been ridden fast, rather than far. Let's just rub you down a mite and we'll talk about it some more in the morning."

The pony's hide was already fairly dry. If Handsome Luke had left it saddled after a long hard ride the damage was already done. He'd find out, come morning, whether the poor brute had caught a chill or not. He spread the saddle blanket over the planking to dry, barred the stall behind the pony's rump, and left it in the dark to stiffen up or prove how tough it was on its own.

As he walked back to the house he saw the kitchen windows were glowing friendly. As he mounted the back steps he saw the other gal in there was a redhead. Both Mormon gals had their hair unbound almost to their waists. It was hard to tell what kind of a waistline a gal in a shape- less nightgown might have. But both filled the top parts of their thin cotton sleeping duds mighty interesting. The red- head had the bigger pair. On the other hand, the blonde's looked more sassy with their nipples poking so inside the cotton, as if they were trying to bore holes through the same.

As he stepped inside, the blonde he'd already met introduced herself as Miss Della, and the redhead was the Widow Fran. Longarm introduced himself in turn. Both widows sat him down at their lye-bleached pine table and took turns putting plates of cold but tasty grub in front of him. As he inhaled cold beans covered with sugar and vinegar Miss Fran said she was sorry they had no coffee, but added that she didn't mind if he smoked, as long as he promised not to kiss her, afterwards.

He didn't know how to answer that, so he didn't. Miss Della blushed and flustered, "Don't tease the poor gentile, Fran. Outsiders don't understand our saintly humor, so watch your saintly manners."

The redhead's nipples were starting to show, too, as she made a wry face and allowed most men joshed the same, whether they'd read the Book or not.

To change the subject, Longarm said, "I've read it. Your own prophet makes about as much sense as most, no offense. But while we're on the subject, I do recall Brother Joseph Smith allowing the American Indian to be the Lost Tribes of Israel, right?"

The Widow Della looked pained and said, "Only one of them, and I have my own reservations about *Paiute*. In all justice to Brother Joseph, I don't think he raised much poultry. Why would you care whether we consider redskins Jewish or not? Don't you gentiles have enough crazy things to say about us?"

"I forgot to mention I ride for Uncle Sam," Longarm said, "who don't much care whether Indians are Jewish or not, as long as nobody is bothering 'em without a hunting license. We got complaints about Indians as well as white settlers being worried by mysterious riders, out this way. I don't suppose you ladies would know if your temple was sore at them Skull Valley wards of the Great White Father this summer?"

The redhead refilled his glass with lemonade as the blonde widow told him, "We don't hear much from the Salt Lake temple these days, since they've gotten so newfangled. Fran and me are content with the old-time religion, the way it was before those so-called progressives in the big city got to fretting about Utah, or Deseret, as *we* prefer to call it, being admitted to the silly old Union."

The redhead placed some sponge cake in front of him as she chimed in, "The Danites have never pestered the Indians out here, much. It was usually pesky gentile settlers they had to run out of Deseret and, like Della says, they've been trying to get along better with outsiders, since Brother Brigham decreed that the law of the land should be followed, even by saints."

The blonde agreed. "There never was much Danite riding in these parts, even when the army was persecuting us so mean. Me and Fran was just little girls when the army made a martyr out of poor dear Brother Lee, of course. But we'd have noticed if any of our elders had been mixed up in that misunderstanding. So we can tell you nothing like that ever went on around here."

Longarm muttered that was nice to hear as he dug into their sponge cake. He was too polite to say the War and Justice departments had understood exactly why they'd hung the ferocious Mormon leader, Brother Lee. There wasn't anything, even in the Book of Mormon, that gave anyone the right to dress up like Indians and attack gentile wagon trains. Some saints held that Brother Lee had shown pure saintly charity when he'd spared those children, wiping out that wagon train at Mountain Meadows. The army had considered the testimony of those sudden orphans sufficient evidence to hang the war-painted white man behind the massacre. But Longarm knew better than to argue about religion or the war between the states. So he washed the last of the cake down with lemonade and said, "I didn't think any of you saints were bothering the Paiute. Maybe the agent up to Skull Valley can tell me who might be. I don't mind telling you ladies I'm confused about this mission. All they typed up for me was that I was to look into rumors of both red and white folk being pestered in these here parts and, to date, the only human being I've met who's been pestered by anyone would be myself."

He shook his head in polite refusal as Miss Fran started to cut him another slice of cake and said, more soberly, "I can see I'm keeping you ladies up past your bedtime. So to end this discussion sensible and simple, I'd like you to consider one last question."

They both looked down at him attentively. So he said, "Please don't take this wrong. But I have noticed in the past that some of you out-of-the-way saints who don't get into Salt Lake City often might not see fit to report each and every thing you may be worried about to the main temple. What I'm getting at is that settlers of your persuasion who may or may not be having trouble with local night riders might or might not see fit to report it to the territorial law in Salt Lake. Are you with me so far?"

The redhead said, "I doubt it. Those of us who still follow the old ways know how to deal with persecution from Salt Lake or anywhere else. If any saints in these parts felt menaced by anyone, the last place on earth they'd report it to would be the U.S. government. So whoever might have sent for you could hardly have been a saint."

The blonde nodded and said, "Any gentile settlers who thought someone was after them would have, loudly, and no doubt they'd have never said it was a mystery. There's not a gentile in these parts who can watch a range fire without blaming it on our church and all the Avenging Angels we're supposed to send after all our neighbors."

Longarm sighed and said, "I've noticed that. So who could be left?"

Miss Della shrugged and said, "Don't look at us. This is

the first we've heard of trouble in these parts. Would you like me to show you to your room now?"

Longarm apologized for keeping them up so late and rose from the table to put his dishes in the sink. Miss Della said she was surprised to see he was married, and led him out of the kitchen with her candle. He wondered, as he followed, whether she knew how much of her he could see, through that thin cotton, as she held the light on the far side.

She led him into a small sweet-smelling bedroom off the main hall, lit another candle for him by the big feather bed, and told him the sanitary facilities were down the hall and to the right. He'd seen by the lack of an outhouse, out back, they had indoor plumbing. It wouldn't have been polite to ask how they managed so fancy on poultry and an occasional boarder. As if she'd read his mind, she said, "You'll find the bed linens new, all the way from Chicago. Our late husband left us well provided for with mining stock as well as his insurance." Then she sighed and added, "It was the least he could do, if he had to ride so fast everywhere he went."

Mention of mining stock dredged up a whole new line of thought for Longarm. But they were both on their feet and he, at least, had had a mighty long day. So he told her he could hardly wait to get under that fine patchwork quilt, and she moved back into the hall to let him do so.

He hung up his hat and coat, draped the gun-rig handy over a bedpost, and tucked the derringer between the headboard and the mattress before he got down to serious undressing. He could see there was no key in the lock across the room. But, hell, what were the odds two Mormon widows had been lying in wait for him all this time? He hadn't known he'd be staying here himself, until he got this far.

He stripped to the buff, got under the covers, and snuffed the bedside candle. The pillows smelled of sachet, and the crisp new sheets felt so good against his naked hide

61

they almost gave him a hard-on. He yawned luxuriously and closed his eyes. Then he heard the door latch snap quietly and opened them wide again.

He decided not to go for his gun, after all, when a female voice asked him, softly, if he was still awake. He allowed he was, and without any further shilly-shally, whoever she was got in bed with him. Then she said, "Oh, you don't have anything on."

He grinned in the dark as he gathered her into his bare arms, whispering, "It saves time, at times like these, ah, ma'am?"

She just giggled and snuggled closer, hauling her own thin gown up around her middle with her free hand as they kissed hard, and she reached down between them to see what else he might have on. Since what she grasped, gently but firmly, was already on about as hard as it could get on such short notice, she giggled and whispered, "Lord have mercy, is all that for little old me?"

He announced it surely was, whoever she was, and they went deliciously insane together for a spell. It hardly seemed to matter, before he came in her the first time, just who he might be doing this with. But as they settled down for a more relaxed friendly lope in her love saddle, Longarm just couldn't figure a decent way to find out which widow he was in bed with. He knew she'd be offended if he lit a smoke as an excuse to peek. As he started to get inspired again it didn't seem to really matter. She was giving him a fine time, no matter what color the hair he was parting with his old organ-grinder might be. Her naked breasts didn't tell him, even after he'd persuaded her to strip entire. For though he'd noticed in the kitchen that the redhead seemed more busty, the blonde had hardly been flat-chested and, in the dark, they'd no doubt both feel grand. Hers did, whichever one she was. But though he tried to just enjoy what heaven had sent his way, his curious nature pestered him to decide whether he was getting all these sweet kisses and skillful bumps from the pretty but cool-looking blonde or the sultry and more sassy red-head. Recalling her uncalled for teasing in the kitchen, and how she'd made her co-widow blush, he decided it had to be old Fran. So there he was, picturing a pretty and well-padded Fran as he made love to her in the dark, when the door opened again and the redhead he'd thought he was aboard came in with a lit candle to say, calmly, "You might have waited, Della. I told you it was my turn, this time."

The thinner blonde Longarm was caught in the act with grinned up, roguishly, and said, "Oh, don't be jealous, Fran. I'm sure there's enough here for the both of us."

That was true, Longarm found, as Fran left the candle burning and stripped to the buff before joining them in bed. For by this time they'd kicked off the covers entire and it was hard to say which one of the young and obviously lonely widows had the nicer figure. Since he'd already pleasured the blonde, Longarm thought it only fair to roll aboard the redhead as she moaned about how selfish Miss Della was. Longarm could see, once he got started with Fran, why Della might have felt she needed a head start. For he'd been right about her having more padding on her chest, and she wasn't built at all bad where it really counted, either. It seemed impossible anything between a gal's legs could feel better than where he'd just been. But, if only because it was so new and hence arousing, he felt inspired to treat old Fran just the way she kept begging him to treat her, as the blonde sat up to regard them both re-proachfully and say, "Hurry, hurry, that looks so wicked I just can't wait to do it some more!"

She behaved as if that were true, once it was her turn again. But Longarm had noticed in the past that situations like this got to be more scandalous than pleasurable, once everybody got to showing off as much or more as they were enjoying it. He knew most men, and doubtless most women, daydreamed about three in a tub when they were hard-up and alone. But once such dreams came true, in real life, a man who didn't want to be called a sissy had downright sweaty work on his hands. Or maybe *hands* were not the parts he had to worry about. It was easy enough to play with one gal while one did it right to another, and that, at least, gave a poor brute a head start when it was her turn again.

But there came a time—Longarm had lost count—when he simply had to unkink his spine, stretch out on his back between 'em, and say, "I surrender, dears. Far be it from me to speak ill of the dead, or to call a lady a liar. But you both know damn well that no man born of mortal woman could do this regular, or even more than once a week." Then, as one or the other gave a playful tug on his limp privates, he sighed and amended it to maybe twice a week, adding, "'Fess up, you young gals have been saving up for a victim like me, right?"

Fran laughed, but the blonde pouted and said, "I guess we know who the *victims* might be around here. No *saint* would have taken such cruel advantage of poor widow women."

He cocked an eyebrow and said, "That's likely true. I doubt either of you would have been so forward if I hadn't been an outsider you figured for a lost sinner to begin with. I surely wish I'd sinned with more coffee, earlier. For, no bull, honies, you've about wore me out for the night."

Fran giggled and said, "Sinning with sinners don't count. Our beloved Hank is waiting in the great beyond for us, to treat us right eternal. But here on earth, we're stuck with such few sins as we can manage and, oh, Custis, you'd be surprised how many passing strangers are shy about starting up with widowed saints."

Longarm assured her he'd assumed as much. Della sniffed and said, "I wish you wouldn't call this sinning, Fran. It's tobacco and other gentile vices the prophet warned us against. He didn't say there was anything wrong with normal pleasures of the flesh, as long as they're not adulterous."

Fran sat up, stretched, and said, "I know. I've always wondered what it would feel like to really sin. But so far I've not had many chances." Then she smiled in sudden inspiration and asked Longarm, "Custis, do you have any cigars on you?"

"Hardly *on* me," he said. "But I have some cheroots in my vest. What did you have in mind?"

"Sinning. Not serious sinning. I don't want to go to hell. But on the other hand, it hardly seems fair to expect a gal to die a pure goody two-shoes. Light me a cheroot and let me try something I've often wondered about."

As Longarm sat up to grope for his duds the blonde rolled off the bed, protesting, "Stop it! I won't be party to such wicked goings-on, Fran."

But the redhead insisted and so Longarm, now knowing exactly what they were arguing about, got out a cheroot and lit it from the candle flame as the blonde stamped her bare feet and told them they were both behaving horridly.

Longarm enjoyed a drag on his cheroot. He'd almost forgotten how good tobacco tasted after lemonade and a lot of kissing. He asked Fran what happened next and she said, "Lay back. I want to get on top and smoke and screw you at the same time."

He did. She did. And Della ran out of the room, bawling that she couldn't abide such dirty doings. So as she slammed the door after her, Fran handed the cheroot down to Longarm, saying, "It tastes disgusting. Put it out and do me right some more."

He did, snuffing the candle as well before he rolled atop her with a laugh to ask her, "Did you just do that to get rid of poor old Della?"

And as Fran entwined him in her loving arms and long legs she giggled and said, "Yep. Don't it seem nicer in the dark with one partner, so romantic?"

He had to agree it did, since it was true. But just the same, when they woke up around four in the morning, doing it some more, he couldn't help wondering whether old Della might not have been an interesting change of pace.

Chapter 6

He never saw the blonde again, and the redhead seemed subdued as she served him ham and eggs by the cold gray light of dawn. He was used to cold gray dawns. So when she pleaded with him not to ever mention to a living soul what might have just happened he assured her his lips were sealed forever. He knew, and he knew that she knew, the Book of Mormon didn't offer a word of justification for the wild night they'd just spent. Neither did the Koran or any other Good Book. But while he'd yet to spend a night in a Turkish harem, he'd had many a lady of other persuasions who'd sort of assumed their Lord wouldn't mind a little slap-and-tickle if they prayed for forgiveness, afterward.

Longarm didn't try to bargain his way out of such occasions. As a lawman, he'd seen enough to suspect hell was full up with real sinners, as long as he didn't do anything really dirty to the sweet little things.

A few minutes later, as he saddled the black pony out back, he told it, "There's something to be said for being a gelding, pard. You just wouldn't understand half the trouble my uncut privates have gotten me into since I first figured out what they were for. Suffice it to say I fear we've worn out our welcome around here. I know we wired the home office we'd stick around until noon. But meanwhile it's fine riding weather, nothing interesting seems to be going on in this one-saloon town, and I won more in the way of expense money, getting here, than Billy Vail is likely to send me in a month of Sundays."

As he led the pony out to the roadway and mounted up he added, "We can check with Western Union later tonight, if we don't find nothing out on the range. Old Billy may not have gotten the night letter yet, in any case."

He was wrong. For as he rode north out of town that morning Marshal Vail had already read Longarm's message and found it more than confusing. Nobody ever got to the office as early as Billy Vail, but Henry was always a close second. So as the pasty-faced young dude reported in, Billy Vail yelled, "I just now got a wire from Longarm, saying he's in Vernon, Utah. How come?"

Henry shot him a puzzled look and replied, "That's where we sent him, sir."

"You mean that's where *you* must have sent him," Vail snapped, "you butter-fingered waste of the taxpayers' hard-earned money! I never told you to type up travel orders to any goddamned Vernon. I told you I wanted him to go to *Vernal,* with an *al* not an *on* on the end of it. Vernal is a hundred and fifty miles closer to Denver than Vernon, you idiot. At six cents a mile that snipe hunt we sent Longarm on figures to cost us dear, and I've a good mind to dock it from your infernal salary, hear?"

But Henry was made of sterner stuff than he looked these days, having been forced to associate with Billy Vail's more ferocious looking deputies until he'd learned to cuss in self-defense. So he said, "If you dock my pay again you can find yourself another underpaid clerk to shuffle your damned old papers. It's not my fault you dictate travel orders with a durned old cigar in your teeth. What difference does it make where we sent Longarm in the first place, seeing it was only to get him out of town until that shooting in the Parthenon blew over?"

Vail growled, "Six cents a mile, and it's already blown. I caught up with Judge Culpepper in the Buckhorn last night, gave him a good Masonic handshake, and he agreed it was just plain dumb to issue an arrest warrant on the shooting of a menace to the community like MacTavish."

He ejected a thick stinky cloud of cigar smoke at Henry and patted his ample paunch as he added, "I got the restraining order right here in my vest. So it's time to get Longarm home and back to work. Since he ain't where I sent him. Send him a message to come back in from Vernon, along with the usual mileage and per diem. The poor cuss must be confused as hell right now. I knew them cow thieves around Vernal had been rounded up before I sent him over to the Green River country. But at least he'd have heard they had, and felt free to head on home. Lord only knows what he thinks of my brains right now, poking about another range entire. I sent him to a quiet neck of the woods, deliberately. But sending a deputy to the sheep and sage flats around *Vernon* is pure *ridiculous*. Neither screwing a sheep or an extra wife comes under federal statutes, and that's about the extent of crime in them parts."

Henry thought and decided, "If I know Longarm, and there's nothing going on in Vernon, he'll likely head next for the nearby Indian reserve. We told him we'd had complaints about Indians being threatened, remember?"

Vail grimaced and said, "Hell, I meant Utes, up in the Green River headwaters. The diggers further west, where you sent Longarm, have never complained about anything. The nearest reserve out of Vernon would be Skull Valley. I can't see Longarm riding that far for no good reason. But send him a wire there as well. I can't have my senior deputy wandering about out there on vacation when this office is so shorthanded."

Longarm was a mile or more north of Vernon, on the trail that more or less followed the barely wet stream some old-timer with a lot of imagination had decided to call Cherry Creek. Like its more famous namesake running through Denver, it watered far more cottonwood and scrub willow than wild chokecherries. But the far west was a mite over-stocked with Cottonwood and Willow Creeks, so what the hell. Nobody but digger Indians and small boys ever bothered to really look for wild chokecherries.

But the trail would go on up to Bingham Canyon and other hard-rock camps near the Great Salt Lake. It vexed him a mite to see the telegraph line part company with the trail as he kept riding north. But he didn't find it mysterious. Copper wire cost money. So Western Union strung its lines as straight as possible and, crossing sage flats, this was straight indeed. The trail meant for man and beast to follow naturally stayed closer to such water as there was in such dry country. About an hour out of town he reined the black pony over to the creek and let it drink and nibble some streamside greens as he rested it. He knew they'd be using the water bags soon enough. He wasn't looking forward to the taste of warm, rubber-scented water. So he lay flat, upstream, and inhaled some of Cherry Creek as well.

They rode on and did the same twice more. Then the damned trail forked. Longarm reined in to study on that. Both ways leading on to the north looked about as well traveled, or maybe as seldom used, this far from anywhere. He spied a sunflower windmill way up the trail leading away from the stream. He knew it hadn't sprouted natural above the sage. So he headed that way, hoping for directions even if coffee and cake was too much to hope for in Mormon country.

As he rode closer, he could see the spread consisted of a whitewashed frame and an orchard of low-slung apple and peach trees that had no business growing in such dry country. As he rode into the dooryard a bearded gent and over a dozen women and children came out on the veranda to gawk at him as if he were a circus parade. He couldn't tell how many of the more mature-figured gals might be wives or daughters of the prosperous nester. The sturdy middle-aged Mormon didn't tell him as he stepped down off the veranda to wave him in about as friendly as a gent packing a ten gauge in the other hand could. Longarm remained in the saddle as he waved back and said, "Hold your fire. I'm the law and it's perfectly legal to grow peaches on a sage flat if you got that much ambition."

The Mormon allowed he had six or eight head of cattle grazing here and about as well, and lowered his shotgun muzzle more politely as he asked what else Longarm might want to know.

The mounted deputy said, "I'm investigating rumors about you folks having trouble out this way. You'd know better than me if anyone was pestering your peaches of late."

The Mormon looked sincerely puzzled as he replied, "I can't say we've had any trouble we can't handle ourselves, friend."

Longarm said he could see that was a ten gauge and the burly nester glanced down as if surprised to see he was holding it as he explained, "A man has to use common sense when none of his boys are full-grown yet. But to tell the truth you're the first stranger we've seen since yesterday, and he never stopped."

Longarm sighed and said, "I wish he had. I just hate guessing games. I don't suppose you could at least describe him to me?"

"Sure I could," the Mormon said. "He was dressed sort of Mex and riding a pony that could have been the twin of that black gelding of your own. We howdied him and he waved back polite enough. But he seemed to be in a hurry. He never even slowed down."

71

Longarm nodded and said, "I suspect I know who he was and where he was bound for. You say he came down this trail from the north?"

When the nester agreed Longarm asked, "From *where*, then? I'm a stranger in these parts and there ain't no town on the map this side of the Skull Valley reserve."

The helpful Mormon explained, "I'm not sure you'd want to call any of the settlements along the apron of the Cedar Range *towns*. But let's see, there's Miss Mildred's general store and post office a few miles on. Then there's the four or five families sort of clustered around the mouth of Cedar Wash and, oh, yes, there's that construction camp half a day's ride this side of the Indian agency. They're laying out some new irrigation, just east of the mountains."

Longarm shot a glance at the dusty but thriving orchard off to one side and said, "You saints sure irrigate a lot. But far be it from me to say you don't know what you're doing. This land was all surveyed as the Great American Desert until you folk come west to prove the government survey teams wrong."

The Mormon's chest expanded a mite as he modestly murmured, "It's a shame the Book doesn't hold with wagering money. For a gentile scout named James Bridger once offered to bet Brother Brigham a dollar against every ear of corn anyone could grow out here in the Great Basin. It wasn't easy. The seagulls helped us with the crickets and we still had to dig and dam like beavers. But in the end James Bridger had to eat crow, as well as all the fine produce we sold the army, once the Mormon Wars were over."

Longarm hadn't come all this way to hear the now-familiar brag of the Latter-Day Saints. So he cut the nester off with, "I just said I admired folk willing to work as hard as they could dream, sir. I reckon I'll ride on as far as that Mormon irrigation project, and if they tell me they're not having any trouble I may as well ride back this way again. I don't know why folk spread false rumors, but they do."

He was about to swing his pony around when the Mormon he'd been jawing with said, "The people laying out that new irrigation are gentiles, not saints."

Longarm reined in again to raise an eyebrow and ask, "Do tell? I thought you folk had a sort of monopoly on making this here desert blossom as the rose. Does Salt Lake City know outsiders are watering the former nation of Deseret, this close to your Mormon Delta?"

The nester who seemed to get by well enough on one wind pump grimaced and said, "We live in changing times. Our elders say we have to live and let live, if ever we're to become a state. We're not that close to the Mormon Delta, out this way, and a lot of gentiles have filed homestead claims in these parts. I'd be fibbing sinful if I told you I *liked* the notion. We could have stayed back east if we'd want our children growing up amid the temptations of your world, and I hope you'll take that more friendly than it may sound."

Longarm said he was well aware of the persecutions that had driven the Mormons over the South Pass back in the '40s, and then he said, "I hope *you* won't get insulted, neither. But ain't it a fact that in the old days some night riders of your persuasion did their best to discourage others from settling out this way?"

The older man shrugged and replied, "They did. I might or then again I might not have ridden with them on occasion. But as I just told you, this Salt Lake temple has forbidden that sort of thing since we've applied for statehood. It's a simple fact that the U.S. government, not our territorial government, has the final say about homestead claims. It was your own Brother Abe, not our Brother Brigham, who passed that infernal homestead act back in the sixties. Don't ask me why. Some of the newcomers who've been granted homestead claims out here don't even speak English. But there's nothing we can do about it and, looking on the bright side, how many gentiles can tempt my growing daughters in Basque or Swedish, even if they settle close?"

Longarm chuckled, wished the poor man luck with his

73

neighbors, and rode on. He didn't see any neighbors for a good four or five dusty miles. Then he spotted a tin roof top baking in the sunlight up the trail and, when he finally got to it, he saw it was a big-frame general store with smaller shacks and a corral back off the trail, as if more shy. Another somewhat narrower trail ran west from the juncture in front of the store. It was rutted enough to qualify as a wagon trace. By standing in his stirrups Longarm could make out the purple ridges of the Cedar Ranges over yonder. It made more sense for a store to be located here, where settlers from the mountains came down to meet the main trail, if he was on a main trail.

He dismounted out front and tethered his pony to a porch post. As he moved up the sun-bleached plank steps the screen door popped open and a pretty enough though no-longer-young lady told him he was a sight for sore eyes and asked in what way she might serve him. Longarm didn't want every Mormon gal in the territory mad at him, so he said he was in the market for some camping supplies and soda pop, if she had any.

She led him inside and told him root beer, warm, was the best she could do, adding, "I stock tea and coffee for my gentile customers, of course. But I fear I never brew any myself. I had some ice in the root beer barrel, oh, about a week or so ago. But I fear the last of it's run out for this year."

He said he'd pass on warm root beer and, knowing better than to ask for real beer, said he needed a canvas tarp, a couple of flannel blankets, and at least one tin pot. When she suggested a frying pan he shook his head politely and said, "Not in such dry country, ma'am. I can't spare the water to scour greased-up utensils with wet sand. I've found you can cook most anything in a pot with maybe a pint of water, as long as you leave it in the cans. I'm going to need some coffee, canned beans, tomato preserves, and maybe some pemmican or smoked salami, if you stock it."

She said she sure did and added, "I can see by your diet

you must be a cowboy. Are you looking for work or do you have something lined up with that irrigation company to the north?"

He told her he was the law and let her get started with his order before he said, casually, "I used to work cows, when I came west after the war from West Virginia. That's where I got used to eating so reasonably on the trail. It's funny you should ask if I was looking for such work around here though. I don't recall no big gentile beef out-fits in these parts, and I fail to see why an irrigation outfit would be signing cowhands on."

She got down the blankets as she told him, "I was being sort of polite, not knowing you were the law. It's been my experience that gents who pack six-guns for a living usually dress sort of cow. I sold some tobacco and a warm meal, just yesterday, to a passing stranger who wore his gun as seriously as you, and he was outfitted so cowboy he could have passed for a Mex vaquero."

Longarm nodded and said, "I may have met him down in Vernon, if we're talking about silver conchas down his pants legs, ma'am. You say that irrigation outfit has been collecting hired guns?"

She proceeded to line up canned grub on the counter between them as she replied, "Not in so many words. But as you might have supposed, hardly anyone rides through here from Vernon without stopping for at least a drink of water and directions. So I've found it hard not to notice that a lot of strangers have been on their way up to that construction camp of late and, while one of them said he was an engineer, and all of them have been polite, I couldn't help noticing at least a couple of tie-down holsters and a certain wariness I know of old. You see, my late husband was a lawman, too. We came down here from Bingham when he retired. Bought this business with his pension. Even so, he had that look in his eyes until the day he died, peacefully, with neither his gun nor his boots on."

She reached under the counter for a baled pot, almost

slammed it down by his canned grub, and added half to herself, "I thought once he hung up his gun he'd lose that cat-eyed way of staring at strangers and unexpected noises. But he never, and I don't mind telling you it's might upsetting to a woman to have her man throw down on her every time she drops a dish in the kitchen."

He smiled crookedly and said, "So I've been told. That's why I don't mean to marry up until after I retire, if then. Can we talk some more about spooky-eyed gents on their way to irrigate sage flats? I know lots of construction outfits feel a certain need for armed guards and such. But how often do the Sioux hit an irrigation ditch, even if this was hostile Indian country?"

"We've never had Indian trouble around here," she said. "We know better than to cut down their piñon trees over in the Cedar Ranges, and they know better than to mess with our livestock. We saints got along with them even before the BIA came out from Washington to herd them closer to Skull Valley. Diggers may go after food, sort of casual, but not when they're well fed by the BIA, and you're right about no Indian at all being out to raid an irrigation ditch. They've plenty of water over in the hills. That's where the new irrigation project is getting it."

Longarm frowned thoughtfully, started to ask a dumb question, and decided they'd be able to answer it better at the Indian agency. The BIA would surely know if someone was out to steal Indian water rights. They'd be the first ones to bitch about it, loud, and send for the army instead of a deputy marshal, while they were at it. All the range that wasn't already claimed between Vernon and the big lake had to be federal. That irrigation outfit would have to have a federal permit if it was digging enough ditches to matter. Riding that far was likely a sheer waste of time. But he had no place better to look for the folk who'd asked Billy Vail for help.

As he helped the Mormon lady pack his purchase into a neat possibles roll, he couldn't help but wonder if he was wasting some of his own hard-won money. None of the locals he'd met so far seemed to need any help with sinister strangers and some, such as this nice old gal, had to be more helpless than a construction company that had been sending away for serious help. So who, or what, could be threatening a whole mess of armed men while it left scattered settlers alone?

The storekeeper looked alone indeed as she asked him whether he might not want to wait under her roof until the overhead sun cooled off a mite. He said, truthfully enough, that he purely hated to ride on, but that he had to. He knew she'd be hurt if he added he thought she was built mighty nice for such a good old gal. So he didn't. The sacrifices he was called upon to make for the Justice Department were a crying shame. But a man just did what he'd been sent to do, and Billy Vail hadn't sent him all the way out here to comfort *every* widow he might meet.

Chapter 7

As he continued north the trail kept trending west toward the Cedar Ranges. Longarm didn't mind, seeing he was already so far from the other trail along the creek. He knew the trail he was following now was more likely to meet up with water of its own as it got closer to the mountains, if that was what anyone wanted to call the Cedar Ranges.

Utah was divided almost down the middle by serious ranges sort of tucked between the Continental Divide and the great dry basin, reaching all the way to the California Sierras. But this far west of Utah's real mountains, ranges like the Cedars stood as sort of islands surrounded by seas of dead-flat, dry country, sage and even grass-covered this far east, giving way to ever drier range and salt flats as one trended west to the deserts of Nevada. The hard-working Mormons had first settled along the aprons of the higher mountains east of a fault line making up the so-called Mormon Delta, running down from the east shore of the Great Salt Lake to the headwaters of the Sevier River, a mightier stream than Cherry Creek, but doomed to die of thirst in the salty desert. Longarm figured the Cedar Ranges to his left to rise a good forty miles or so west of the irrigated Mormon spreads around Utah Lake, a fresh-water feeder of the big salty one. So newcomers irrigating this far out were a hard day's ride from enough Mormons to have a serious war with. The ones he'd met out this way so far seemed content to get along with gentile neighbors. But that didn't mean any number with certain reservations about the matter had seen fit to tell a gentile lawman how they *really* felt, and of course some outsiders could have their own doubts about the Mormons they were moving in with.

Longarm had found most of the sect decent enough, save a few ultraconservatives that even worried the Salt Lake temple with their own interpretation of the Angel Moroni's views about getting along with outsiders. Most of the trouble between the Mormons and outsiders sprang from odd notions spread, and even published, by folk who didn't try to understand why they'd come out here in the first place. Longarm was fair-minded enough to take them at their word when they said they were Christians, even if, like John Calvin, the Prophet Joseph Smith had sort of had some further notions on the subject. A Mormon lady had assured him, and he'd seen no reason to disbelieve such a nice gal, that the widely published penny dreadful about some other gal being forced into joining old Brother Brigham's harem against her will had been a crock of bull. Sir Richard Burton, the English spy and travel writer, had published a book more favorable to the Latter-day Saints, and it had still made some of 'em mad as hell. So Longarm figured it was only fair to take that with a grain of salt as well. He'd spent at least as much time in Salt Lake City as any Englishman just passing through might have and, so far, he hadn't noticed anyone kidnapping gentile gals off the streets or gunning outsiders just for smoking. Salt Lake City was a lot like Denver, except for having the mountains rising the wrong way behind it. He knew for a fact you could get just as drunk and in just about as much trouble in either town. Save for all the published exposés and the suspicions such reading put in some folks' heads, someone just passing through a Mormon town of any size would hardly notice he wasn't in a regular old American town. It was outsiders, on the prod, who started most of the fights, and that Mormon lady back at the crossroads store had told him a mess of outsiders, packing guns, were up the trail a ways.

As he walked his pony, Longarm got out the orders old Henry had typed up to see if he'd missed anything about a construction outfit. It didn't take him long to see he hadn't. There were only three pages, and the last one was half-empty. He'd been sent on many a mission on many a fuzzy tip, but this one had the others beat all hollow. Henry hadn't even put down the names of anyone calling on Uncle Sam for help. His orders simply read that he was to look into local rumors, for God's sake, about mysterious night riding and sinister strangers seen drifting about with no visible means of support. He swore and put the onionskins away again, muttering, "I can go down to Larimer Street any night and see more gents with no visible means of support than I could shake a stick at!"

The only strangers anyone had been able to tell him about out here, except for the late Handsome Luke, *had* visible means, if that construction outfit was hiring gun hands. There was nothing too unlawful sounding about that. The railroads, mining outfits, and even big beef spreads tended to have some hard-cased hairpins on their payrolls, lest someone mess with them. A construction outfit would have all sorts of tools, dynamite, and such that wandering saddle tramps might be tempted to steal. They'd have a payroll to worry about as well, unless they knew some way to make gents dig ditches in hot dry country for free.

It was getting hotter and drier as he rode on. He was tempted to turn back. But he never. For Handsome Luke had come down this very trail, with the expressed intent of murdering a man he knew by name. So, somewhere to the north, the son of a bitch who'd *sent* the rascal had to be still alive and waiting for word on how Handsome Luke had made out. Longarm was anxious to tell him, and ask him how come, if only he could figure out who and where he might be.

The trail dipped across a dry wash running west to east down from the now much higher ridges to his left. Longarm was not surprised to find the sandy bottom dry as sand could get, this late in the year. But he could tell by the cottonwoods thriving along either side of the wash that the water table wasn't too far down, even in summer. Unlike mesquite, cottonwood couldn't manage where its roots had to run down deeper than five or six feet. He crossed over and was about to go on when he spied thin wispy smoke rising through the tree branches between him and the Cedar Ranges. That was something to study on. It made sense to camp in the high country to the west. It made sense to camp along the trail down here on the sage flats. But nobody would be camping that far up a dry streambed, unless they didn't want to be noticed from the trail.

Longarm circled back, dismounted, and tethered his black pony to a tree before he hauled out Handsome Luke's Winchester, levered a round into the chamber, and mosied upstream to see what might be seen.

He got the drop on them easy. The smoke was rising from a small thrifty fire four Indians had built on the flat bed of the wash, around a bend that hid them from the trail. They had no horses, or much in the way of duds, for that matter. Longarm surmised the old man, middle-aged woman, and two younger gals had to be a digger family, off the reservation a good ways.

The younger gal spotted Longarm first and went stiff, muttering in Ho through frozen lips. The old man turned his head, sighed, and got to his feet as he raised both

81

empty hands and said, in passable English, "Do not kill us. We have nothing, nothing, and we are not evil people."

As Longarm moved closer, lowering the muzzle of the Winchester politely, the old digger added, "If you wish to screw one of my daughters I won't fight you. I have nothing to fight you with. It would be wrong to kill us for no reason."

Longarm got out two cheroots as he joined the frightened family around the fire. He saw they'd been cooking a jackrabbit on the coals. He said, "If my Ho brother would like to smoke with me, I have some food aboard my pony. I can see you are a good hunter, but that rabbit won't be enough for four Ho to get indigestion out of."

The old man reached gingerly for the smoke Longarm offered him, saying, "You are right. But what can we do? They kill us if we hunt their sheep, and the sheep have driven all the antelope away. It makes my heart soar to see you wish to smoke with me. How are you called and how is it that you call us Ho? Most of you people call us Paitute, Goshute, all kinds of Utes, even though the Utes call us worse things and kill us."

Longarm said, "I call Sioux *Lakota* for the same reasons. I was brung up polite and it's rude to call folk things they might not call themselves."

The older man hunkered down to light his gift with a brand from their fire as he rattled off a quick assurance to the three women, who looked at least a mite less worried about Longarm now. The one who had frozen even smiled at him before she lowered her eyes and looked away. The old man got back to his feet, enjoying a deep drag as Longarm lit his own smoke with a match. He saw the envious look the old woman shot up at him and handed the old man a half dozen matches, saying, "Your woman may have some use for these, someday when her fire drill is damp."

The old man nodded soberly and said, "Hear me, I hate most of you people. But I think you are not as bad as some of them. We are smoking together, like men. I am Weet-

82

zuka. I know it is rude to get to the point so soon, but we are hungry, hungry. Did you mean what you said about sharing food with us?"

Longarm told them to wait right there and left to go get his pony. When he led it back to them the old Indian noticed he'd put the rifle back in its boot. He wiped at his leathery face and barked a curt order to the women when they started to rise, looking as if they meant to eat pony and all. Longarm unlashed the possibles roll, spread it out on the sand, and handed each Indian a can of beans as he opened it with his pocketknife's can-opener blade. He had to give them credit when he noticed none of them dove in before all four had been rationed. Weetzuka asked what Longarm meant to eat, and as soon as he was assured Longarm had no hunger, all four diggers demolished their pork and beans without bothering to chew.

Then they tore the rabbit apart and swallowed that as well. As the old man chewed the juice from a leg bone and spat it in the dusty sand, he rubbed his bare belly and said, "Those little brown nuts were very good. Which one of my daughters do you want to enjoy now?"

"They're both so pretty I dare not risk offending the other by choosing one," Longarm said. "And making love to *both* would *kill* me. But seeing as you also feel so friendly now, I wonder if you could tell me the answers to some questions."

Weetzuka said, "Gladly, if I knew anything. But we are not from these hunting grounds. The Great White Father brought us here from our old lands to the west and tried to make us live at Skull Valley. No real people would want to live at Skull Valley. They make women wear cotton dresses there. That makes them catch the lung sickness. We tried to tell the agent that. He said we had to wear clothes anyway. It was terrible. I just got over the rash around my waist and crotch. It is better to live as we have always lived, if only there was more game around here."

"I figured you for reservation jumpers," Longarm said.

"But I don't ride for the BIA, and so as long as you're not hurting or scaring nobody, I've no objections. You're the ones who figure to wind up hurting. You're all too right about game being sort of scarce once cows and sheep move in."

He took a thoughtful drag on his cheroot before he said, "Hear me. I've been sent to look into stories about evil strangers bothering red and white folk in these parts. Aside from making you wear pants, has anyone been bothering you, old son?"

The naked digger shook his head and replied, "Not the way they used to, when all the wagons were coming through before my daughters were born. They told us the Great White Father says it is wrong to use Ho just for target practice. I think this must be so. Nobody has shot at me for a long time now."

Longarm said, "The few settlers I've spoken to say there's been no Indian trouble in these parts recently. What can you tell me about those new settlers, digging irrigation ditches between here and the reserve you all ran away from?"

Weetzuka shrugged and said, "We passed through the hilly place where they have been making a big beaver pond in a canyon. We had hunger. I hid my women and went closer to see if they wanted to kill me or give me some food. A man with a gun asked what I was doing there. When I told him I had hunger and two daughters he could screw he laughed, led me over to a chuck wagon, and asked a fat man wearing an apron to give a sack of flour to the poor old monkey. What is a monkey?"

"Something like a tree squirrel," Longarm said. "That's as close as I can come without drawing pictures. In other words, the crew up yonder treated you no worse and even somewhat better than most rough-and-ready white men usually do?"

"I think so. The flour lasted us almost a week, and I think that was kind of them, don't you?"

84

Longarm nodded and said, "Sounds like old hands at outdoor work who ain't looking for trouble with Indians if it can be at all avoided. You say the guard you met had a gun. If he wasn't on the prod for, well, diggers, no offense, he must have been on the prod for somebody else. Would you be able to say, for sure, whether you all were the only kind of Indians around here?"

Weetzuka shook his head and said, "Yes and no. I told you they were crazy, crazy, at the Skull Valley agency. All the people the Great White Father has gathered there speak Ho. Maybe he thinks they are all one people. But he has gathered in bands who don't all live the same way. Some of them were enemies in the days before you Saltu came out here to confuse us even more. Some of the Ho at Skull Valley are what you people call Horse Utes or Shoshone. Some are even trying to live white. Ho look dumb in boots and big Saltu hats. But I have to be fair to the agent at Skull Valley. He has forbidden fighting between bands. Nobody who speaks Ho has been out raiding this summer. I just ran off with my women because, as I told you, reservation life makes my crotch itch."

Longarm pointed west and asked, "What about Indians roaming the high ridges over yonder after piñon nuts and such?"

The old Indian said, "Not at this time of the year. Not this far from the agency at any time if you are talking about *tame* Ho."

Longarm asked what about wild ones and the old digger struck a proud pose as he replied, "We are the only ones around here who are not feeding from the hand of the Great White Father. It is not easy to get by in such picked-over country as this."

Longarm nodded and said, "I can see even the livestock have to stay spread out amongst all this yummy sage."

Weetzuka frowned and said, "Saltu sheep and cows don't eat sage unless they are starving. They search for the funny grass and other weeds you people brought in with your boots and wagon wheels. Didn't you know that?"

"Yep," Longarm said, "I keep forgetting you folk don't savvy dry humor much. I have to ride on now. So I want you all to listen sharp."

Only the old man could, but the three women watched with considerable interest as Longarm set aside four more cans and rolled everything else back together in his tarp, growling, "I'm leaving you more than I ought to because I was brung up Christian. I know it ain't enough because I've crossed hard country before. If you haven't figured out by this time that it's time to head back to your agency, old son, you're just dumb as hell. So whether you survive another four cans worth before you all dry up and blow away, or whether you make it back to Skull Valley sort of hungry, is academic. I've done as much for you as I can. There's nothing in the U.S. Constitution that says all five of us have to go hungry just because you read clocks backward."

Weetzuka said he didn't know how to read clock dials in either direction. So Longarm suggested, "Start looking at the sun more sensible, then. When you see it rising in the west and setting in the east, you'll know time is running backward. While it's still running forward, you'd best give up this fool notion of going back to a life that was hard enough when you Ho had this great basin all to yourselves."

The old man protested, "Hear me, my dream spirits tell me the old ways are the only ways for a real person to live."

So Longarm stood up to lash his roll back in place aboard the black pony as he said, "Your dream spirits are full of shit, then. I can't say I admire the way this old world keeps changing under me. I used to get my cheroots two for a penny, and my job was less dangerous before double-action six-guns came on the market. I liked things better when gals wore their bodices more low-cut, and I just can't stand riding into that new barb wire after dark.

But this old world keeps turning and it just don't care if we want to keep up with it or not."

He swung himself up in the saddle before he added, in a gentler tone, "I know an Arapaho in Denver who's taught himself to be a barber, and he makes a fair living at it. Your daughters are young and pretty. You owe it to them to let 'em get some proper duds and book-learning. There's just no future for bare-ass and illiterate old women in this country, now."

Chapter 8

Longarm sort of proved his point a few miles on up the trail when he came to another crossroads hamlet hunkered under another windmill. As he watered the black pony from the galvanized tank the windmill fed, when the wind was blowing, a barefoot white gal in a flour-sack shift came out of the nearby frame shack to tell him that would be a dime for his brute, or two bits if he meant to refill his water bags as well.

Longarm dismounted, reaching into his pocket, as he told the wispy little blonde that his water bags didn't need filling just yet. Then he asked where he was and she said, "We calls this Spike's Place. Before you ask, we don't know just who Spike might have been. Mammy and Pappy found this place ghosted when the Mormons run 'em out of Vernon a few years back. A sign above the door of yonder shack said Spike's. Pappy figures it used to be a store, from the shelves and all. He fixed the windmill and we got eighty or ninety head watering from it now. That's why we got to charge for water. We don't make real money on that."

Longarm handed her the dime anyway and asked if they sold provisions out of the old store these days. She shook her head and said, "Not hardly. Mammy will feed you if you want to come on in and give her fifty cents. My sister, Susannah, will do more than that for a dollar, but I don't go in for that sort of stuff with strangers."

She dropped the dime down the front of her shift, and added that was about the size of the services for sale at Spike's Place. Longarm managed not to grimace as he allowed it was early for supping or screwing, but asked, "Would you folk have done business with another gent aboard a black pony, just like this one, recently?"

The whispy gal nodded and said, "Sure. He said he was called Handsome Luke. Susannah said it would cost him a dollar anyways. I don't know whether they was just funning or not. Pappy gives her a licking when she does it in front of anyone. He was through here yesterday as a matter of fact. Said he'd just rid down from that irrigation project in the hills to the north."

Longarm frowned thoughtfully and asked if the hired gun had said whether he'd been working for the construction company or only ridden through. She said they hadn't asked. So he asked how she and her kin felt about the irrigation scheme.

She shrugged and said, "It ain't our business. We got enough water for our stock, if we keeps an eye on it. Pappy says he ain't cut out to be a farmer, and that if he was he'd farm sensible, where it rains more often. Why pay for watering corn when the good Lord is willing to water if for you free, further east?"

"Folk farming semi-desert more or less have to pay more than that for water, ma'am," Longarm said. "Would you happen to know the rates that irrigation outfit is asking for an acre-foot?"

She shook her head, then grinned sheepishly and said,

"I know that other gent on a black pony opined a dime a drink seemed a mite steep. So they must be charging less, up yonder."

That didn't really help. Irrigation water could run steep as hell and still look almost free in modest amounts. Growing crops used up hundreds of times their own weight in water. So a price that might strike a stock raiser as reasonable could break a homesteader trying to show a profit on a quarter section of farm produce. He asked the raggedy little blonde whether the construction crew or anyone else had been giving her and her kin any worries. When she just looked blank and asked why anyone on earth would want to pester poor but honest folk in the middle of nowhere, he remounted and quit while he was ahead by bidding her good day and riding on.

He rode until the rooftops behind him were out of sight and then swung off the trail to the west. He'd established more than once that Handsome Luke had been sent down that trail to head him off. It might be safer, or at least more interesting, to approach that irrigation project from an unexpected angle. So far, they sounded too reasonable to be sending hired guns out after anyone. But whether Handsome Luke had left from their camp to begin with, or simply passed through it from the north, any big construction camp in out-of-the-way places tended to turn into small towns with all sorts of small-town grifters lurking about. He didn't want to ride in aboard Handsome Luke's pony and silver-mounted saddle until he had a better notion of how many whores and gamblers, or worse, might remember Handsome Luke fondly in and about that camp.

He knew he was turning an easy day's ride into a more considerable expedition by zigging and zagging and jawing so much with everyone he met. But thanks to Billy Vail's vague orders it couldn't be helped. Just beelining in like a big-ass bird could be risky enough when a lawman knew exactly who he was after and what sort of backup the rascal might have. Henry had failed to even type up the direction to go, once he got to Vernon. He'd gotten in enough trouble just stopping there and only finding out that somebody, somewhere, didn't want him going a step further.

His detour toward the Cedar Ranges started well enough, except for the time he was losing on his way to more important places. From time to time he met a scrub cow, too intent on survival to charge him. The cheat grass growing between the clumps of sage was, like the tumbleweed, an almost useless species introduced from the old world by the white man. It was well named. It grew where more sensible grass couldn't grow, green and sudden, after any kind of rain at any time the ground wasn't outright frozen. Cheat grass sprouted along railroad banks, atop sterile slag heaps and mine tailings, or through the pavement of downtown Denver if you didn't watch out. But once it shot up and went to seed within days, cheat grass was a piss-poor imitation of the real thing. There was so little nutrition in its air-filled dry stems that a cow had to eat it by the ton to keep from starving to death. There was plenty of it all around out here, but the poor skinny brutes he passed were in the position of a man trying to live on celery. They used up about as much energy as cheat grass provided just chewing so much of it.

He noticed none of the skinny and doubtless tough beef he passed wore the same brand. But if those people at Spike's Place had been run out of more settled range, the local law likely knew of their casual views on property, and brand inspection was not a duty of the Justice Department, so what the hell.

As he topped a gentle rise he looked back to see the top of their windmill was still barely in sight. He knew none of their stock would drift much further toward the mountains. Few cows were smart enough to figure that a ridgeline rising in the distance might mean water and better grazing.

The infernal ridgeline just kept hanging there against the cloudless cobalt sky as he kept riding toward it. But the range was commencing to roll up and down under his

91

pony's steel-shod hooves now, so he knew they were getting closer to the aprons of the Cedars, even if the damned range did seem to keep sliding westward every time they dipped down into a draw.

The sun was in his face as well now. But after a while he noticed the heights ahead were more brown than purple, and that there was even a salt and pepper dusting of boulders and trees along the skyline. More serious brush began to rise above the sage around them. He patted his mount's neck and said, "It won't be long, pard. I'll rest you under a juniper, cropping real grass or at least rabbit-brush, if only you'll carry me on to the promised land."

Then they topped another rise and he muttered, "Shit," as he saw a big mud pie of talus staring him in the face. He reined more to his left, explaining, "It's out of our way north, pard. But it would be even slower getting there if I busted one of your legs clambering up that treacherous runoff fan. That much talus adds up to a damned old box canyon, anyway. We'd best make for the ridges beyond the easy way south, and if we wind up camping out tonight we wind up camping out tonight. Damn those hungry Indians."

It got even worse before it got better. Like most of the north–south ranges of the Great Basin, this one was a casebook study of erosion gone loco, at least on the lower slope where rare but serious rainwater was free to plow hell out of soil and soft rock unprotected by vegetation. They had to zigzag all over hell, even turning back more than once, before they made it up to the first beach.

Longarm had had many an argument about that. A lot of folk who passed through these parts aboard wagons or trains refused to believe there could be *beaches* in such dry country, even when one pointed out the shelves that ran along the hillsides surrounding the Great Salt Lake. But once upon a time, at least two swamping inland seas had filled a good part of the Great Basin, draining north to the Snake over passes that were now eighty or more feet above the level of the present lake and salt flats. Some Swiss scientific gent back east had allowed the west had been a lot wetter, way back when. Longarm would have known he was following a sandy beach north even if he'd never read *Scientific American* in the Denver Library when his pals weren't looking. The sandy strip was fifty or more feet wide, dropping off to long-gone watery depths to his right, and bounded by a wave-cut cliff to his left. From time to time he even spotted shells imbedded in the sand ahead. They looked new, as if the surf had cast them up on the last high tide, if inland seas had high tides. He couldn't say whether they were real seashells or fresh-water mussels. It was hard enough just picturing all those sage flats to the east under eighty feet of water, without wondering whether it had been salt or fresh. He figured there must have been at least some salt in it, long ago, considering how salty what was left of the long-gone bigger body of water was.

They loped a spell, making up the lost time in the afternoon shade of the cliff to their west. Then they rounded a bend and Longarm said, "Shit," again as he reined in. For the way ahead was blocked by a slide of house-sized boulders from higher up.

He dismounted, filled his hat from one of the water bags, and told his pony as he watered it, "That's what we get for trying to follow such old seashores. It figures to be cooler and greener higher up, and there's always a game trail along the ridges."

Then he poured another hatful of water over himself, drank some of it, and put on his refreshingly cool hat again, saying, "I'd best walk you back a spell. We got to find us a crack in the wall to get higher."

They did, losing another hour or more in the process, and the pony never would have let Longarm lead it up such a narrow, steep slot if it hadn't been for that Spanish bit. When they finally made it up to gentler slopes, paved with bunchgrass and dotted with juniper, Longarm comforted his pouting pony by feeding it a big chaw of greenery, and even led it on foot a spell to make up for dragging it over boulders like that.

They crossed another wave-cut shelf, carved out when the prehistoric sea had been even higher, and then they found the going easier for a few miles, even though the slopes were a mite too steep for Longarm to mount up again.

When, at last, they busted through some scrub cedar to see the land beyond dropped off to the west, sort of scary, Longarm told his mount, "I said it would be cooler up here. Don't that west wind feel fine? You just go on and inhale some grass while I look for that game trail I told you about."

He tethered the black pony to a wind-tortured cedar surrounded by grass and Mormon tea and, sure enough, he found a fairly well beaten albeit narrow trail trending north more or less along the line that parted rainfall, east or west. The timber grew thicker down the west slope, since that was the side that got the most water, when and if any came down. He knew a lot of the greenery up here got by mostly on mountain mist. Clouds tended to scrape their guts on ridges, even when the flats below were going cobweb dry.

Having gotten his bearings, Longarm removed his coat and hat to flop in the grass near his grazing pony to rest his bones long enough for a well-deserved smoke. He didn't see how they'd make it much farther north before sundown, and riding over unfamiliar mountains even early at night was asking for more bum luck than he felt up to. He decided they'd make camp at the first good fort-up they came to. This one was all right for a trail break, but too exposed to build a fire. He knew he'd need a fire before morning at this altitude. It was hard to believe how hot it had been down there on those sage flats, even staring down at 'em through thoughtful smoke rings.

The country he'd just ridden up from had seemed hot and dry enough. Off to the west, purer desert shimmered under the afternoon sun and, near the horizon, a greenhorn in these parts would have been sure he was looking at an arm of the Great Salt Lake. But Longarm knew what a mirage was. It had been one hell of a time since the Great Salt Desert over that way had been under water for real. Now it was just a dead, flat expanse of dirty-white rock salt, pure enough to sprinkle on your steak, if you could take a little grit with your beef. He tried not to think about steak, gritty or not, as he remembered giving all his beans to those fool Indians. He still had plenty of canned tomatoes, and there was still the chance he might bark a squirrel before supper time. The old digger had been all too right about piñon nuts up here. He'd only passed a few such trees so far, and none of them had been bearing ripe cones.

He finished his smoke, got back to his feet, and untethered the black pony, muttering, "I wish I could eat grass. But what the hell, I've gone a week without grub in my time and I'm still here. Let's get on up the ridge while there's still plenty of light left."

They did. Each time they topped a high stretch Longarm stared hopefully north. But if there was anything interesting that way there were too many infernal trees blocking his view. A lot of landmarks west of, say, Kansas, had been named sort of dumb. But the old-timers who'd decided this was a cedar ridge had known what they were naming. It was too bad most of the rain hit the high massif from the salt desert side. But enough leaked over the lee of the ridges to grow considerable timber down the east slope as well and, of course, that outfit wouldn't be digging irrigation ditches down that slope if they'd found it *really* dry. He decided they'd likely considered the wetter side first and given up on it because no amount of irrigation water was going to help the salt flats to the west.

The trail led down into a low grassy saddle. Longarm was just idly wondering why no cedar seemed to be growing in the gap when a sheepdog barking in the distance explained it to him. The dog, a small but ferocious-sounding black and tan mutt, was bobbing down the far slope toward him with apparently murderous intent. What had looked at first like scattered gray boulders across the way began to act like sheep as they gathered together in the way sheep will, whether they've a sensible reason or not. Longarm just hated to shoot dogs. So he peered about for the human in charge of all this rapidly-moving livestock. There had to be a sheepherder with a herd of sheep. The State of Colorado gave a man a year at hard labor for abandoning sheep on the range. Lord only knew what Utah Territory had to say about the crime. Utah took sheep more serious than Colorado.

The yapping sheepdog was coming up-slope at him now. Longarm drew his six-gun and called out, "Hold her right there, dog." But the little beast kept coming. He wasn't certain it was out to bite his pony's legs. But the pony was on Longarm's side, the strange cur wasn't, and so it was about to catch a .44-40 round in its snarling fangs when the air was rent by a whistle shrill enough to hurt Longarm's ears and spook his mount.

Longarm forgave the insult to his eardrums and the few crow hops his pony made down the slope when he saw the sheepdog stop as if it had been grabbed by the tail. Then it spun on a dime and ran back even faster than it had been coming, toward a barely-visible figure standing near the tree line on the far side of the meadow-filled saddle.

Longarm nodded and muttered, "That's better," as he holstered his six-gun and rode on down and across. He hadn't gone far before a vagrant shift of mountain breeze shoved the smell of sheep up his nose. He grimaced and rode on anyway. Longarm was fair-minded about sheep, for a former cowhand. He knew that smelling sheep, to a cowhand, was a lot like smelling an Indian camp if you'd been raised white. Neither sheep nor Indians really gave off worse smells than cows or white folk. It was all in what you were used to inhaling. Longarm had noticed, traveling a lot by train, that prissy-dressed folk from big cities sort of looked upset when a good old boy off a cow spread sat down next to them. A friendly Chinese had once assured Longarm that to *them*, Americans in general smelled like rancid butter. There'd been no call for him to get so sore when Longarm had said *he* smelled sort of like a sweaty sardine. Nobody could help what they smelled like, as long as it wasn't plain old dirt.

As he rode up the far slope he could see the sheepherder was a female. She was dressed a lot like a Navajo lady, so he knew she had to be Basque. They were too far north for Navajo, and everyone knew the Navajo had copied their current fashions from Basque herders brought in by the Spanish when they still owned the southwest states and territories. As he closed the distance between them he saw she was not only too pale-faced to be Navajo, but was packing a Henry repeater as well. As the black and tan mutt fell slavishly in the shade of her dark skirts she levered a round into the chamber of her rifle and called out to him, "That's close enough for now. State your name and business on my range, stranger."

He reined in to call back, "I'd be Deputy U.S. Marshal Custis Long, and since this is federal range I don't reckon we ought to argue about who ought to be on it, ma'am. I admire your good grasp of English, but, ah, maybe I'd best talk to your men folk?"

She replied, sort of sullen, "My father is not here. He is far to the south with our main herd. There is too much timber on this thrice-accursed range. I am called Felicidad Laxalt. My people came from Montalban in the land the French and Spanish stole from us. Can you prove you are a lawman? You do not look like a lawman."

Longarm got out his wallet and held it open so the sun could glint off his federal badge at her. She was, of course, too far off to read his I.D., but maybe she didn't know how to read anyway, for she said, "All right. I didn't think a Mormon Danite would have a cheroot gripped in his teeth like that to begin with. I have a pot of stew on the fire near my cart. If you have any coffee we may have a deal. I hate to herd in country where they say it is a sin to drink coffee. Thank God I don't dip snuff as most sheepherders do."

He chuckled and told her, "I got half a can of real Arbuckle coffee and some tomato preserves as well."

"Good, I have sugar to sprinkle on your tomatoes for our dessert. Follow me."

He did. It wasn't easy, aboard a pony, since she had to duck some cedar branches leading him into the woods on foot. Then they made it to a small clearing on flat ground, well screened on all sides by trees and boulders. A two-wheeled canvas-covered cart leaned on its shafts near a small fire with a big witchy pot bubbling on the coals. As Longarm dismounted he asked idly where her cart pony might be. She said, "My father took it with him after posting me here. I think he is worried about my running away with a handsome Mormon."

It would have been impolite to ask the young gal how often she ran off with anybody. So Longarm led his own pony across the clearing, tethered it to a piñon, and unsaddled it. Then he toted the saddle back to the fire and broke out his own contributions to their supper while she fed her dog some raw scraps and talked to it in Basque, a lingo that was so odd Longarm couldn't get the drift of a single word.

He noticed her English was almost pure American as they sat across the boiling pot from one another, jawing about this and that as the shadows got longer and the pot kept smelling better. Longarm didn't mind the smell of sheep as long as it was dead and cooked. And she smelled more like a schoolmarm than a sheepherder. Aside from letting her fool dog do most of the herding she'd obviously been at some soap and water as well as violet toilet water, mighty recently. It might not have bothered him as much if her heart-shaped face had been ugly or if she wasn't hunkered on her bare heels with her skirts so careless. She ladled out two tin plates of lamb stew and said they'd have the sugared tomatoes and coffee later, explaining, "We like to make meals last into the night and it's still early."

He dug in to find he hadn't known how hungry he was until her hearty stew commenced to stick to his ribs. Like most raised country, Longarm usually tended to eat serious and talk later. But she was a talk-and-eater, and he wanted to make the good times last. So between bites he questioned her about the mysterious troubles in this neck of the woods.

She said she hadn't heard of any trouble out this way. He had to allow her kin would hardly leave a pretty young gal, and sheep they might value as well, alone in these hills without even a pony to call her own if things got exciting. She said her kind got on well enough with the local Mormons and that she hadn't seen any Indians at all that summer. He asked what she knew about that big irrigation scheme to their north and she told him, "They're all right. I got whistled at by some pick-and-shovel hands when my father and me passed through from the north with our herd. But they weren't serious. Lord knows how many painted women they have in their mushroom town at the mouth of the canyon they're damming. My father says whores and gamblers always follow such action. But for a boom town it's said to be sedate enough. The colonel has lots of hired guns to keep his workers safe from the drifters and vice versa."

Longarm swallowed a mouthful of stew, wishing the coffee was ready, and asked who and what her colonel might be. Felicidad shrugged and said, "That's what they call the man in charge up there. Don't ask me why. I've never even seen him. A Basque who was doing some ditching for him told my father the colonel ran a big project over in Nevada a few years ago and didn't screw his workmen out of their pay. That's all the Basque knew about him, but to a working man who doesn't speak much English, that's enough."

Longarm smiled thinly and said, "If it's any comfort to

you, I once drove a herd many a mile for a rascal that failed to pay us off at the rail yards in Dodge, and all of us spoke English good enough. The slicker still got away with all our back wages. Your Basque pal didn't say how well the project itself seems to be going, did he?"

She looked puzzled and asked, "Why would the colonel have so many men digging all those ditches if he didn't like the way it was going? I told you nobody in these parts have even heard of those mysterious riders in your orders, Custis. The man we spoke to would have surely told us if the construction company was being pestered by anyone, no?"

He nodded but said, "Try it the other way. Old Jesse James is said to still be mad at the Missouri Pacific Railroad because of the way they built roughshod across the land of poor white kin. That's no doubt just an excuse on Jesse's part, but there have been cases of big outfits pushing little folk about. More than one small spread standing in the way of progress has been burnt out mysteriously by night riders unknown."

She shook her head as she reached behind her for her coffee pot, saying, "There weren't many settlers up that way to begin with, and the ones there were have been making money hand over fist, selling produce and such to the big construction crew and their hangers-on. More have moved in, since the promise of water got around. The colonel would be dumb to run off nesters, even if he was a mean old crook. What's the sense of irrigating dry land if you don't let people settle it?"

As she put the pot on to heat up, Longarm lit a cheroot before he mused, half to himself, "Water sure is valuable in sagebrush country. I've investigated many an ugly dispute over water rights. In a land where men have killed for a canteen of water, a nester holding rights to a spring or even the riparian rights to an all-year creek could find himself in a whole lot of trouble."

Felicidad shook her head and said, "There's nothing like

100

that going on. These hills wouldn't be so timbered if there wasn't so much groundwater. It crops out as springs all up and down the range. The only trouble is that, running down to the flats, it sinks in. I know the spring-fed canyon the colonel is damming. Nobody had ever claimed that water, before he filed on it, that is."

"What about Indians?" Longarm asked.

"They have their own water supply, a good one. An all-year creek runs down Skull Canyon. It dies in the desert, later, of course. But they never would have set up the Skull Canyon agency there if there hadn't been more water than any Indian would ever use. They don't take a bath every day like me."

Longarm stared thoughtfully at her, resisting the impulse to sniff, as he replied, "Do tell? Modern wonders never cease if you have a bath tub in your pony cart, ma'am."

She laughed, reminded him her name was Felicidad, and got to her feet, saying, "Come, I'll show you. I have some naptha soap and, to tell the truth, you don't exactly smell like roses after a hot day in the saddle."

Longarm said he was game for anything that didn't hurt as he got to his own feet. So she took his hand and led him across the clearing and into the trees on the sunset slope. It was only a short way down and around some boulders to a small inviting tarn of cool clear springwater. She said, "We'd better hurry. Once the sun goes down it will be too cold up here." Then, before he'd barely had time to take in the whole scene, let alone figure out what they were doing there, Felicidad had shucked her Basque blouse and skirts to dive headfirst into the tarn, wearing no more than the cake of soap in one hand.

As she came up, laughing, she waved the wet soap at him and said, "Come on in, the water's just right after sitting in the sun all afternoon."

So Longarm sat on a handy boulder to shuck his own

boots and duds as she politely turned away to stare at the sunset to the west.

He was glad she had, by the time he had his pants off. For while she'd only invited him to enjoy a bath with her so far, his fool private parts were sort of rising to the occasion and he could only hope the water was cold enough to simmer 'em down before she noticed. He dove in, opening his eyes underwater to make sure he didn't bust his face on a submerged rock. He saw no rocks worth mention as he breaststroked underwater to join her in the center of the tarn. But the sunset glow that filled the tarn gave him a better and longer view of her naked body than she'd offered in her sudden strip and dive. So it wasn't cold enough to cool his pesky erection, after all.

He still might have managed to behave himself, seeing she was likely just young and unsophisticated about skinny-dipping with strangers. But then she insisted on soaping him, all over, and as they stood face to face in the sunset she only observed he sure was muscular, until she got to soaping him further down, blinked in pleased surprise, and closed her eyes to murmur low and growly, "Oh, yes, that's just what I've been praying for, night after night, up this goddamned mountain!"

She was kind of young, and he knew how Basques felt about men of any breed messing with their women. But since any Basque who spotted him bare-ass in this tarn with her was likely to get just as mad in any case, it seemed only polite to take her in his arms before *she* could get mad at him as well.

She didn't *get* mad but she *went* sort of mad as she floated her bare submerged legs up to lock around his waist. She let go the soap to grasp his intent and guide it where they both intended it to be a spell. He waded her, that way, to where he could brace his palms against a boulder with his bare feet on the sandy bottom and her bare bottom gyrating amazing as hell under the water. He didn't have to move his own hips at all, even though he did, kissing her hard as she tried to twist his hard-on in directions it just wouldn't go. They climaxed almost at once. She never even slowed down. But she did let him breathe, at least. So with his wet lips brushing hers he chuckled and said, "I hope you understand I never would have started this. For, no offense, I took you for somewhat younger when we first met this evening."

She hugged him closer and purred, "I was afraid you'd dismiss me as a foolish virgin and, as I said, a girl doesn't get to meet many men, herding sheep."

He laughed and said, "Yeah, *boy* sheepherders get a better break that way."

She almost snarled, "Don't I know that, and can't I guess why Poppa prefers to herd alone! It's just not fair. He thinks he's preserving me for an old friend from back home in Montalban. I keep telling him and telling him I consider myself an American girl, but he insists on keeping me almost a prisoner, up in these hills."

Longarm couldn't answer until he'd come in her some more. Then he chuckled and said, "From the way you move I'd have to say you haven't been kept in solitary confinement as much as your daddy might hope."

She giggled and said, "Where there's a will there's a way. I just love to do this, don't you?"

"I wouldn't be doing it if it hurt," he said. "Please don't get cold gray afterthoughts on me before sundown, honey. You don't have to justify your natural feelings to me. I've been getting the same ones, ever since I found out why boys and girls was built so different."

She said, "Good. Let's go back to the fire and do this right, all night, in your bedroll. I get a thrill from strange bedding as well as strange bed partners. Do you think I could be some sort of sex maniac?"

"Lord," he said, "I sure hope so." And so they got out of the tarn, naked, and walked back to the fire hand in hand, carrying their duds with their other hands. By the time they got there the evening breeze across the ridges had goose-bumped them. So it was fun warming up in his bed-roll and they just never got around to making any coffee or dessert that night.

Chapter 9

Longarm was sorry they hadn't when Felicidad shook him awake around four in the morning. He wiped his sleep-gummed eyes with a hand and protested, "Hold the thought until I can wake up, for Pete's sake. You gals have an advantage when it comes to screwing half asleep."

She hissed, "Someone's coming! I fear it's my father with the rest of our herd, since my own dog is not attacking."

That woke him up. As the wayward Bo-Peep rolled bare-ass out one side to get dressed, fast, Longarm threw all his own stuff on the blankets and tarp, gathered the corners into a Santa Claus bundle, and ran bare of foot and behind across the clearing with the bundle in one hand and the silver-mounted saddle in the other. He didn't look back when he got to the black pony, untethered it, and led it north into the tall timber with his hands full and the reins gripped between his teeth. By the time they were a good rifle shot from Felicidad's camp Longarm was laughing at

105

the picture he had to be presenting to the birds they kept flushing. So he stopped, took time to at least saddle the pony, and rode on like a Lakota brave seeking a vision, with the big bundle on his bare back. A mile or so north along the ridge he felt safe to fort up among some boulders and get dressed. As he buckled his .44-40 back on and hunkered to roll his bedding right, he sighed and muttered, "Women sure like to live dangerous. I ain't had such a close call since that fool husband walked in on me and that Denver gal who neglected to inform gents she picked up at church socials she was married."

By this time the eastern sky was a disgusting oyster gray between the cedar branches. He lashed the roll back in place, mounted up again, and rode on, telling the pony, "I'll water you once we know for sure a herd of sheep ain't on our trail. I'm sure old Felicidád will come up with a good explanation for those extra cans and all my coffee, should her daddy notice. Next to husbands, you just can't beat strict fathers for suspecting the innocent and missing the obvious."

By the time the sun was all the way up Longarm felt sure he was in the clear, wherever he was. So when the trail led them down off the main ridge to where a rill of springwater ran east-northeast across a green mountain meadow Longarm reined in, got down, and let the pony enjoy some water and grass while he had a cheroot for breakfast. That infernal Basque gal had wound up with the last of his provisions as well as his virtue.

As the pony grazed Longarm explored further down and saw someone had dammed the creek with a small but expensive watergate of timber and store-bought hardware. It was set to let the rill run on down to wherever, at its current level, while the vertical sheet of boilerplate would back up sudden flooding occasioned by the serious rain, and let the results run on down more gradually. A steel wheel standing waist-high above the knee-high watergate controlled the flow. Longarm looked all about, didn't see a soul who might object, and proceeded to shut the watergate entire. He and old Felicidad had sweat together some since that unexpected and enjoyable skinny-dip in that mountain tarn, and there was just no telling when or where he'd get a better chance to clean up a mite.

Closing the watergate naturally resulted in a rapidly growing pool of backed-up rill. He walked back upstream to the grazing pony and made sure it wouldn't run off on him. Then he went back to sit on the grass and haul off his duds again. He spread his gun rig on the grass, closest to the little pool he'd just manufactured, and, knowing what he was in for, jumped in all at once.

He'd been right. The pool was less than three feet deep and so cold it took his breath away at first. But he ducked his head down between his frigid knees to get wet and blue all over. As he came up for air and warmth, running his fingers through his sopping hair, he was suddenly aware a strange white man was playing cigar-store Indian by the watergate wheel. He had one hand on the wheel and the other resting, casual, on the grips of his own six-gun. He was dressed cow, save for the laced engineer's boots and brass badge pinned to the front of his tan shirt. As their eyes met, Longarm nodded, sitting in the ice water, and said, "Morning. I ain't an escaped lunatic. I just needed a bath and, seeing this was so handy—"

"I hope you ain't too dirty," the other man cut in, explaining, "that's *drinking* water you're soaking your ass in. If you're done, I'd best open this sluice again. I was wondering why the water wasn't running, lower down."

Longarm said it was jake by him, and the guardian of the water proceeded to crank the watergate back open as Longarm got out and commenced to get dressed again. It made him feel sort of dumb, and he noticed the other gent didn't go away, even when he had the rill running right again. As Longarm got to his feet, stomping life back into his frozen feet, he introduced himself to the stranger, who took it calmly and told Longarm, "I'm Wes Reynolds. I work for the Interstate Irrigation Trust. You was just bathing in their water on their claim. They have water rights to all the headwaters of Shoshone Creek."

Longarm moved closer to offer the guard a smoke and, as they both lit up, he said, "I don't have no Shoshone Creek in my mental map of these parts, no offense."

"None taken," Reynolds said. "Left to itself, the creek dies out in the sand less than a mile from the hard rock of the foothills to the east. Up to now it's never done anyone any more use than the disgusting Indians it was named for. The outfit I works for hopes to change that by evening out the flow. Left to its fool self, Shoshone Creek can't make up its mind whether it ought to be a trickle dying in the belly of a dry wash or a sudden but short-lived sagebrush swamp. Are you headed for our main camp or did you have somewhere important to go?"

Longarm said, "I might wind up at the Indian reserve further north. But I might as well see all this construction I've heard so much about."

The private guard nodded and said, "Get your pony, then. Mine is just down the slope amid them nut pines. I got to stay up here and make sure some fool don't come along to mess with our watergates. But I can put you on the main trail down to Shoshone. That is what they call our main camp, Shoshone. Dumb name, if you ask me, but once the colonel has all the spreads down that way sipping water through a ditch there won't be no town. So what the hell."

Longarm got his pony and led it politely afoot until the two of them met up with the guard's paint in a piñon grove just down the rill. Then they both mounted up and Reynolds led Longarm what seemed the wrong way until he commented on it. The other rider nodded and said, "You'd have come to a cliff, riding the way you'd think you *ought* to. That's why I said I'd show you the easier way down off this rock pile. The water you just climbed out of don't

108

mind turning into a waterfall, yonder and about, as it works its way down."

They passed through a notch with boulders rising high on either side. Then Reynolds reined in, pointed at a small blue lake ahead, and said, "This is as far as I go. Follow the edge of that reservoir east until you get to its dam. You'll find a canyon trail there that'll take you down to the main camp. Ride at a walk and keep your hands polite until the boys posted near the dam get to know you better, hear?"

Longarm said he knew the rules of dropping in on folk unexpected and added, "I heard you might be having trouble up this way. Is that why you company police are on the prod?"

Reynolds looked sincerely puzzled as he replied, "We're not on the prod. It just wouldn't make much sense for us to be out guarding company property if we just didn't give a damn."

Longarm nodded and said, "I can see troublemakers would start by blowing your main dam if you was expecting any trouble at all, from anybody."

Reynolds assured him, "Hell, we got orders to shoot *beavers* if they mess with the drainage up this way. What's all this about *real* trouble? I'm only drawing a dollar a day and if you mean *Indians,* forget it!"

Longarm shook his head and said, "As far as I know, the local Indians, such as there are, haven't been picking on anyone of late. One of the things I was sent to look into was the other way around. You'd know if any of your construction workers had been fussing with Indians, right?"

Reynolds looked blank and replied, "Sure, but we don't even have no breeds working for IIT. A handful of Mormons, a few Mexicans, and mostly reformed Irish railroad workers is all we have to worry about down to Shoshone Town. The colonel won't even hire Chinamen. We came here to irrigate the desert, not to get in fights. The colonel will fire a worker on the spot for even threatening a fair fistfight."

Longarm agreed that sounded sensible and then he stared harder at the other man's fancy mail-order badge and asked, "You private gun hands ain't Pinkertons, I see. There don't seem to be anything saying what you might be a constable *of*. It just reads Special Constable, period."

Reynolds said, "I noticed that when I put it on a spell back. We're hired direct, by the colonel. That may not mean much to a real lawman with a real badge, like yourself, but you'd be surprised how much easier it is to part two fighting Irishmen when you got any kind of badge at all on."

Longarm chuckled and said, "No I wouldn't. I've been around company towns before. The point of this discussion is that while we both know you're a good old boy, I met a gunslick down to Vernon that had a nastier rep. I was wondering if your outfit made a habit to inquire into the past of its more armed and dangerous looking employees."

Reynolds shrugged and said, "They asked me what experience I'd had as an armed guard. When I told 'em I'd worked here and there as a town deputy or night watchman they said that sounded good enough. I don't know of anybody working as an IIT guard who'd be wanted by the law, if that's what you mean."

Longarm said it was, thanked Reynolds for the help in making her this far, and rode on, pondering what the underpaid rider had just told him. With the price of beef up this year, a top hand could do a mite better than a dollar a day. Of course, an armed guard had a much easier job, provided he wasn't guarding Queen Victoria's crown jewels, or even a bank, and nobody was expecting any real trouble. But, damn it, those orders Henry had typed up said there *was* trouble in these parts. So how come he couldn't seem to find anyone who was having trouble, save his own fool self?

* * *

Billy Vail was giving Henry hell back in Denver because the morning was a little older there, and Western Union hadn't delivered any reply to the callback they'd sent Longarm, day rates, one hell of a ways back.

Henry assured his boss, "I stopped by the telegraph office on my way to work, as you ordered me to, sir. If Longarm had seen fit to reply I'd have brought his wire with me."

"Hell," Vail growled, "I know that. Where in thunder do you reckon that fool could be right now if he didn't even pick up his damn money order?"

Henry said, "Neither in Vernon nor Vernal, if you'd like an educated guess. Neither town is big enough to get lost in. I looked them both up in my atlas last night. Perhaps Longarm has stumbled on to something? You know how nosy he can be, and you did send him to Vernon to look for trouble, you know."

Billy Vail bit down hard on his cigar stub and growled, "Like hell I did. I sent him to *Vernal*. It was *your* fool notion to type in *Vernon,* in another part of Utah Territory entire. And as far as I know, there ain't nothing as exciting as a cake-baking contest going on in either place right now! Do you reckon he could have met up with some female, Henry?"

The clerk sniffed and allowed, "It's happened in the past, Lord knows. But it's odd he didn't pick up the money we sent him, if that's it."

Vail scowled and said, "He never pays for it. I don't know whether that makes him romantic or cheap. How big a town did you say you sent him to by mistake?"

Henry winced and replied, "Population less than two hundred, according to the atlas."

"Women can't be it," Vail decided. "Not even Longarm can screw *all* the time. So if he was still in town at all he'd have dropped by the Western Union by this time. What else did your atlas say might be going on over that way?"

Henry sniffed and said, "The whole *county* only rates a

few lines in any atlas, sir. But I took the liberty of going through our files and asking a few questions at Interior, down the hall, when you made me aware I might have sent Longarm to the wrong part of Utah."

"There was no *may* about it. I'd be even madder if there was anything important going on around either place. What did you find out about Vernon, damn it?"

Henry sighed and said, "Nothing. I'd hardly call Tooele County entire *important*. But at least it's breathing. Their sheriff's department reports the taking of a dead-or-alive dead by some obscure county lawman. The Indian agent at Skull Valley says he's missing a handful of diggers he can afford to spare, but that they don't seem to be bothering anyone. Production at the mostly copper mines along the south shore of their big salt lake is neither up nor down and, oh, yes, Land Management says a few dozen new homestead claims have come in from that area. It seems an irrigation trust is opening up more dry range to farming."

"They're always doing that out Utah way," Vail growled. "Sometimes I suspect Mormons must have beaver blood. Water rights would be territorial, not federal, right?"

Henry made a face and said, "Not in this case, sir. Land Management says that an engineering company is improving the runoff on federal land, with Interior's permission, naturally. Would you like me to ask them for a copy of their claim?"

Vail shook his head and asked, "What for? We ain't the damned Interior Department. If that irrigation project wasn't lawful they'd have yelled to us for help by now. The same applies to them homestead claims. The only time such matters come under our jurisdiction is when somebody cheats. It's up to Interior to make sure they file on federal range, land, water, or minerals, with all the small print right. It would take a Philadelphia lawyer, working overtime, just to read the fool papers Land Management makes everybody fill out before they dare to bust the first sod. If that damn fool Longarm's investigating claims for Interior on my time I'll bust his ass. I told him to go looking for *trouble*, not survey lines that might or might not be off a few yards!"

Henry shrugged and said, "He doesn't really *have* real trouble to look for and, since he hasn't seen fit to drop by the Western Union in Vernon yet, he still doesn't know you sent him out on a snipe hunt just to get him out of the way until you could talk to that judge, sir. You know how he hates to come back empty-handed and so, if I may be so bold as to hazard a guess, I'd say he's just likely to go on hunting snipe, until he *catches* some."

Henry was right, though Longarm didn't know he'd been sent on a snipe hunt, as he spotted two armed guards standing near the dam at the end of the man-made lake and approached them with a friendly wave. They neither waved back nor raised their Winchesters as he rode in, calling out, "I just spoke to your pard, Reynolds, about the way to your main camp, boys."

One just went on scowling at him. The other waved his free hand at the rising sun and said, "Just follow the canyon on down and remember you're on private property if you flush a deer."

The other one scoffed, "Shit, there ain't no deer in these hills," and the other replied, "Trespassers ain't allowed to shoot 'em in any case." Then he asked Longarm, "Did Reynolds ask who you might be, trespasser?"

Longarm identified himself and they both looked more friendly. The one who seemed to know so much about the local flora and fauna said, "You'd be the one they calls Longarm, then. I'm sure proud to meet you. But how come the law would be sending a man of your rep to inspect our dam sites?"

Longarm regarded the low sturdy dam behind them fondly, noting that while it was based on beaver engineering principles, it was built a lot stouter of cedar logs laid with their butts downstream and tops upstream, weighed down with rocks and already starting to seal pretty good with mud, judging from the little water now seaping through between the cleanly sawed ends he could see. A pipeline fashioned of iron-bound cedar staves ran off down to the east from a more serious watergate than he'd messed with higher up, that morning. He said, "I think I see how it works. Are you boys posted here to make sure nobody floods the flats down yonder just for fun?"

The one who'd waved at the canyon trail for him replied, "They ain't supposed to let it run at all until all the ditching is done down yonder. It's a pain in the ass to dig ditches in four or more feet of running water, see?"

Longarm agreed that sounded tedious and rode on down the trail as it dipped below the level of the dam, and the water behind it, to follow what would have been a canyon-bottom creek if nature had still been taking her course. The pipeline ran on the far side, for a few miles. Then it ended, abruptly, and Longarm could see why the upper end was shut and guarded. Loose staves and coil after coil of strap iron showed where construction of the water line had stopped, for now. Naturally no water was running from the open end. It would have been dumb to let it. He was wondering why nobody seemed to be working on the pipeline when he rode through some canyon oak to meet a calico steer, staring his way with a morose expression, tail up and long horns down. As the brute pawed up some dust by way of further greeting, Longarm called out, gently, "Aw, you don't really mean that, seeing as they cut your nuts off some time back." And though it was sort of doubtful the steer understood his words, the tone seemed to reassure it. It let Longarm pass with no further protest.

He passed a few more head of more sedate stock, all wearing the same X/W brand. Then he rounded a curve to spy woodsmoke above a small cedar cabin, set well back from the dry creek bed on higher ground, with the canyon walls rising right behind it. He reined in to study the pleasant scene. The cabin door opened and a pretty little gal in the sort of severe summer dress most old Mormons favored waved to him and shouted, "My man just rid down to the land office, but I can ham and egg you, if you ain't ate yet this morning."

Longarm blessed every black hair on her pretty little head and rode up to dismount and tether his pony as he introduced himself. She said, "Oh, I could see you was a gentile, but I took you for a water company man. Come on in, anyway."

He did. The interior smelled like a clean cedar clothes closet. She sat him at a plank table near her cooking range as she bustled with a cast-iron spider and a big smoked ham that smelled delicious, uncooked, to a man who'd missed out on breakfast by hours. As she busted eggs in as well, he asked her, casually, why her man was at some land office, seeing they had a pretty nice spread that, no offense, looked lived on for a time. Without turning she explained, "We have to move. But my man says we'll come out way ahead. We've never been able to raise more than beef and a few free ranging chickens up this canyon. We only settled here because of the regular water. Now that the water on the sage flats to the east will run all year, we'll be a lot better off with a whole quarter section claim and some produce drilled in."

She turned around to present him with a plate of steaming ham and eggs. He knew better than to ask a Mormon hostess for coffee or even tea. But she ladled out a mug of buttermilk for him, and he had to admit it was a healthy breakfast. To her he said, "Let me see if I get this straight, ma'am. You're abandoning this canyon claim to file on a quarter section of semi-desert?"

She bustled over to a shelf to get down some chocolate cake before he could do serious damage to her ham and eggs, telling him, "The colonel has offered us a much better deal than that. He's swapping us a quarter section of irrigated bottom land free-simple. It won't be semi-desert once its ditched, and they've even offered to move our cabin for us, entire. My man knows more about such matters than me. That's why he rode down to the company land office to sign all the papers. But even I can see what a good deal they're offering. Sometimes, when the water's up in this lonely canyon, it's been sort of frightening. It'll be a lot nicer living on the flats with neighbor ladies within sight."

He washed down the last of the ham with buttermilk as he said, mildly, "You was still getting the water and pretty good forage *free*. I don't suppose you'd know what it's going to cost the two of you to blossom the desert as the rose? There are just two of you, right?"

She ladled more buttermilk at him as if in fear he'd die of thirst with an empty mug as she said, sort of peevishly, "Of course it's only the two of us. Why do you gentiles always ask about that? The Salt Lake temple's been discouraging that sort of thing and, even if it wasn't, a saint has always needed the permit of his first wife to take a second, and it will be a cold day in the devil's domain before I'll have another woman getting in the way of *my* dusting!"

He chuckled and said, "I've heard some Turkish ladies hold the same views, and we was talking about the price of water, ma'am."

She cut him a heroic slice of cake and said, "My man would know what the colonel means to charge for an acre-foot of water. He made them go over it with him more than once before he agreed to swap this holding for a better one. I mean, they had to *show* him it was better. I recall him and the colonel's agent, seated at this very table, discussing something like ripe rights."

Longarm tried some of her cake, allowed it was delicious, and explained, "I think you mean riparian rights, ma'am. Since you and your man was here first, nobody else has the right to dam or divert a stream running across your claim without your permit."

116

She brightened and said, "Oh, yes, that was it. They paid us for them rights and throwed in that quarter section on the flats as well. They said they wanted us outta this canyon in case they wanted to build more dams and flood it, see?"

Longarm frowned and said, "Not really. How much rain could anyone expect on this side of the Cedars? But maybe they know more about flash flooding in these parts than I do. It's none of my concern if you folk are happy with the deal. You're sure neither you nor your man felt, well, *pressured* into giving up this pretty little spread?"

She looked surprised and answered, "Pressured? Good heavens, the colonel is doing everyone in these parts a *favor*. As you'll see when you ride farther down, a lot more settlers are moving in to take advantage of his bounty!"

Longarm grimaced and said, "I'm not certain I'd call it bounty before I see IIT giving all that irrigation water away for nothing. But I reckon a man has the right to make an honest profit. Lord knows the railroads sure did, out this way. I'm not even allowed to do nothing about nine-year-old kids working in coal mines or cotton mills. So you grown-ups are on your own if you get skinned in business deals as long as nobody's pointing a gun to your heads. This sure tasted good, ma'am. How much do I owe you?"

She told him she'd take a broom to his head if he talked dirty to her while her man wasn't home. So he rose to his feet, saying, "Well, I'll just have to settle for telling you I think you're a fine lady, then. I got one more question, and please don't hit me with the broom before you study on my words."

She neither said she would nor wouldn't. So Longarm said, "I can't help noticing you're a mighty handsome woman and that your man still feels safe to leave you up here, alone. I don't mean that fresh. I'm talking like a lawman who's been led to suspect there's been trouble in these parts."

She asked what kind of trouble and he said, "I'll be switched with snakes if I can answer that. If I thought my boss had any sense of humor at all I'd suspect he'd sent me on a snipe hunt. But he's a serious old buzzard and he told me to come out here and make mysterious riders stop bothering folk. Have you been bothered, ma'am?"

She assured him she hadn't, that the few guards and construction workers she got to entertain, with or without her man at home, had been ever-so-polite and decent. So he muttered, "They say nobody's pestering *them* and they don't seem to be pestering anybody *else*. So what's left?"

Then, since she didn't know, either, he rode on.

Chapter 10

Getting down off the Cedar Ranges was a lot easier than getting up into them when one had a canyon trail to follow that cut through all the complications. The sun hadn't made it to high noon by the time Longarm rode into the bitty boom town spread out across the flats from the mouth of said canyon. But after spending some time in the high country the semi-desert felt sticky as hell. He took off his frock coat and lashed it to the saddle skirts with his roll. It made him feel more human, but he seemed to be drawing more stares with his cross-draw rig as he rode along. The camp was laid out neatly, but everything was built of thin planking or just canvas stretched over frames like glorified tents. A place dispensing trade liquor from the keg at two cents a shot was, in fact, a plain old surplus army tent. They were doing a pretty good business, despite the hour. Most of the gents he passed were dressed more construction than cow. But he saw a couple of obvious cowhands as well as farmers in bib overalls and straw hats. Figuring one might know, he asked the way to the nearest Western Union, and when that didn't work he settled for directions to the land office everyone was talking about.

It was set up in a sort of framed circus tent, according to the sign above the entrance. Longarm dismounted and went in. He had to wait in line behind some would-be settlers before the fat gent seated behind a folding map table smiled up at him and asked whether he was interested in crop or range land. Longarm flashed his badge and said, "Neither. I ride for Uncle Sam and I got some questions to ask."

The lot salesman looked calmly surprised as he said, "Ask away then. I'm sure you'll find all our papers in order, ah, Deputy."

Longarm said, "I'm sure I would, too, if I was up to making a lick of sense out of lawyer talk, printed small. Can I take it as given fact that you boys have bought this tract off the Interior Department, with no waiting period?"

The fat man nodded and replied, "You sure can. I'm sure I don't have to tell a federal agent that the homestead act forbids the selling of land that hasn't been settled, improved, and all that bullshit for the required five years. The colonel bought over a hundred square miles of this country off the government for cash, with an option to buy more if his water project works out well."

Longarm nodded and said, "I won't ask what he paid per acre for dry sage flat or what he means to sell it for as irrigated cropland. It's a free country and everyone has a right to get rich as he can. Does this colonel I keep hearing about have a name, and can I take it nobody gets to homestead, a mite farther out, without his permit?"

The lot salesman said, "IIT is the property and brainchild of Colonel Winslow Baxter, late of the Army of Virginia, he says. I rode for the north, myself, but he's a good old boy. As to your other question, you just allowed it's only right for a man to make money by being smart. Naturally, the government won't allow no homestead claims on

120

land they've optioned against the future blooming of this desert. But look at her this way, we're selling good irrigated cropland at less than a hundred dollars an acre, provided you take at least a quarter section at a time, that is. City lots will cost you more and, to be perfectly open and aboveboard, the colonel can't promise you a city here, once all the construction's done. Right now it may look like Dodge with the herds in town. But once we're done, it's up to the locals to vote on an incorporated township and such. The few permanent company hands won't amount to a hundred, counting their families. The colonel figures that ought to be enough to turn the water on and off, maintain the ditches, and such."

Longarm nodded and said, "I noticed there's neither a railroad, telegraph line, nor post office here, so far. How do you folk communicate with the outside world?"

The fat man said, "Easy enough. There's a post office up to the Skull Valley reserve or down at Vernon, if need be. We can always spare a rider, either way. The colonel and his lady are here in camp. So company business ain't all that complicated."

He saw that although some other prospective customers were lining up behind Longarm, the tall deputy didn't look to be going anywhere. So he said, "I'd sure like to chat with you all day. But you'd do better talking with the colonel than me. He knows more about what we're doing here than anyone else, and I'm here to sell land and water, see?"

Longarm asked how much they planned on charging for the water that went with such bargain land and, perhaps because he just didn't know or, more likely because some likely suckers were lined up behind Longarm in the stuffy tent, he said, "Ask the boss. I just work here." So Longarm nodded, said he'd do that, and ducked out.

As he did so, he noticed another company guard with a toy badge admiring his tethered black pony out front. He nodded to the hired gun and said, "Morning. Could you tell me where that colonel of yours might reside?"

The somewhat leaner and meaner looking company gun replied, "I might. I'd rather talk about this horse you rode in on, cowboy."

Longarm got his wallet out again to flash his badge and I.D. as he said, "I used to be a cowboy. Now I take myself more seriously. Has somebody reported a stolen horse answering to this one's description, pard?"

The company gun said, "As a matter of fact, they has. Badger Dawson, the gent as runs the Last Gasp Saloon just down the way, was saying just the other evening that he was missing a black gelding with Morgan lines and a two-hundred-dollar silver-mounted center-fire show saddle. It's a good thing you're the law. For if you wasn't, I'd sure have to ask you a mess of questions regarding this here coincidence, Deputy Long."

Longarm nodded soberly and said, "I find it sort of astounding myself. I'd best have a word with your saloon keeper after I jaw some with your colonel. You'd know better than me where he might be right now."

The company gun said, "Swing right at the next corner and keep going 'til you come to what looks like a frame cottage on wheels. I can't say whether he's to home right now, but that's where him and his lady would be when they is."

Longarm thanked him for the information, mounted up, and rode on to find the colonel's rolling home. It wasn't hard. Nobody else could have afforded to haul such a monstrous whatever out to these sage flats, even if they did build a fair-sized house aboard a sort of stretched out Conestoga chassis. They even had a picket fence around it.

As Longarm tethered the pony to what he saw, up close, to be a picket fence built in sections that likely rode another wagon, the dutch door built into the side of the rolling home opened, or at least the top half did, and a sultry-looking gal wearing her brown hair down and her red terry cloth robe sort of open called out, "He's not here.

Went up in the hills to talk some Mormon out of another cattle spread, most likely."

Longarm opened the gate and walked closer as he took off his Stetson to say, "I must have just missed him, coming down the creek, in that case. Or are we talking about just one creek, Miss, a . . . ?"

"I'm Lavinia Baxter, the colonel's legal playmate. Lord knows how many Mormon gals he has on the side right now. I don't know anything about his infernal construction business. He won't even tell me who he's sleeping with on the side as he rides here, there, and everywhere after whatever. Are those shoulders real? I've never seen a padded work shirt, but on the other hand I've seldom seen a gent built like you, either."

Longarm didn't comment on *her* build, even though she was showing so much of it with that robe sashed so loosely, if at all. He said, "You're likely just fretted by this dry heat down here on the flats, Miss Lavinia. I don't know your man, yet. But as a man who's ridden about some in these parts, I can't say I've seen a flirting gal under *every* clump of sage."

She shrugged, allowing her robe to open even wider, as she asked, "How many women under how many sage-brushes does it take to keep a man out late, night after night?"

Since there was no honest answer that might not upset her even more, Longarm said, "I'd best come back when he's home. You wouldn't know when that might be, would you, ma'am?"

"If I knew that I wouldn't be so pissed, you fool!" she said, and slammed the top of the dutch door shut.

Longarm smiled thinly and went back to his mount, telling it, "You've no idea how much worry they saved you by cutting your fool balls off before you were old enough to worry about female notions, pard. If that old colonel is messing around with some other gals in these parts, I can't wait to see 'em. For he's got a real spitfire, built like one

123

of them statue gals, waiting for him at home all hot and anxious."

He mounted up and headed back to the main drag, pondering on the perfidity of his own sex as well. He knew that many a man with a wife good-looking enough to marry liked to mess about on the side no matter what the other ones looked like. He recalled with some disgust that army officer he'd had to arrest that time for raping a twelve-year-old as well as ugly little Creek gal down in the Indian Nation. The poor bastard's poor wife had stood by him through his trial and all the way to his hanging at Fort Smith, crying fit to bust and pretty as a picture, even wet. The urges of the human critter were just unpredictable as hell. That officer's wife had even given the hangman a hard-on, and yet her man had to go and act so dumb and disgusting.

He asked a passing pick-and-shovel hand directions to the Last Gasp, and as he dismounted out front he discovered once again just how dumb some gents could act. For even though he was getting off the black pony smack in front of its last place of probable legal residence, a fool dressed in black with a silver-mounted buscadero gunrig tore out the swinging doors at him to roar, "That's my horse and saddle, you goddamned horse thief, and now you're going to die, whether you've made peace with your maker or not!"

Longarm stepped clear of the black pony, saying, "Hold your fire. I ain't stealing your horse. I'm trying to give it *back* to you, if it's yours."

"Call me a liar, will you?" gasped the man who could only be Badger Dawson, as he went for both guns. Then he froze and got frog-belly pale when he found himself staring down the muzzle of Longarm's .44-40 with his own guns still halfway stuck in their holsters. He gulped and said, "Well, hell, if you want the pony *that* much, stranger."

Longarm said, "I'm the law. If this is your pony, the man who stole it is already dead. He rode down to Vernon aboard it. I rode it back this way, hoping to run into someone who could tell me more about his recent whereabouts. Does the handle Handsome Luke mean anything to you?"

Badger Dawson said, "Can't say it does. But I can prove that's my pony and saddle. He's got a wire cut on his off shoulder and there's on concha missing, under that roll you seem to have lashed over the skirts."

Longarm nodded and said, "I've noticed both secret signs. If you'll leave them infernal guns alone I'll just take my own gear off and he'll be all yours again."

As he proceeded to do so, the mollified saloon keeper told him, "I reckon I owe you a drink or more, seeing you're so tender-hearted and honest. How come you never gunned me when you beat me to the draw just now? Most gents would love to say they got the one and original Badger Dawson. You've heard of me, of course?"

Longarm shook his head and said, "Nope. If you'd been on my wanted list I might have treated you more serious just now. If you go on acting so loco with total strangers I doubt you'll last long enough to get really famous."

As he removed his possibles, Longarm added he had no place handy to leave 'em. So Dawson said, "Bring 'em inside, then. I'm always ready to do favors for my friends, and I sure like to be friends with gents who draw so sudden. You say you're the law?"

Longarm nodded, identified himself, and Badger Dawson gasped, "Oh, thundering Jesus, I slapped leather on *Longarm* and lived to brag about it? This really calls for some serious drinking, old pal!"

Longarm followed the saloon keeper inside, noting as he did so that the place was almost empty. As the owner told the bucktoothed gal behind the bar to stow Longarm's possibles under it and put some bourbon and branch water on top of it, Longarm told him, "I'd rather have a beer, maybe needled a mite with rye if you got it. And I wish you wouldn't brag too much about our recent misunderstanding, Badger. I know another saloon keeper in Dodge who made up an awesome rep to keep his wilder customers from busting the place up. He hails from New Jersey and must have been worried about being taken for a sissy by the Texas hands who get paid off in Dodge and make a lot of noise about it. His name's Luke Short."

Dawson grinned and said, "I've heard a lot about Luke Short and his famous Long Branch Saloon."

Longarm said, "So have a lot of homicidal lunatics. My point is that poor old Luke Short has attracted so much attention with is rep that he's had to learn to shoot in self-defense a heap. He once told me, personal, that if he had it all to do over again he'd just serve free drinks to gents like the Thompson Brothers and *let* them call him an eastern dude."

As the bucktoothed barmaid slid their drinks at them Longarm tasted their suds, pronounced 'em fit for human consumption, and shot a glance outside, saying, "It's your pony we're talking about, now. But do you reckon leaving him saddled in the noonday sun is likely to do wonders for his speed if you ever have to ride somewhere in a hurry?"

Badger Dawson nodded and called out to an older man leaning on a mop in one corner to go out and tend to his long-lost steed. As the old swamper leaned his mop handle against the far end of the bar and shuffled for the front entrance to do as he'd been told, a younger but almost as shabby individual got up from a corner table, followed the swamper as far as the door for a look-see at the black pony, and then went back to his table and sat down to study his own suds some more. Dawson downed his bourbon, chased it with half the water, and muttered, "Tastes more like soap than branch water. But they say the colonel's fixing to let fly with the main ditch any time now."

Longarm said, "Groundwater's always a mite alkali in these parts. As to ditches full of mountain water in the near future, I'd say we're talking more like six or eight weeks. I just rode down from the reservoir and—"

"Which one?" Dawson cut in, adding, "They got three

canyons dammed so far. I heard the main one up in Willow Canyon's about to get tapped."

Longarm frowned thoughtfully, shrugged, and said, "It's what I get for thinking one modest lake could water all the land staked out down here, I reckon. That accounts for the man in charge not being home just now. How many springs are we jawing about, seeing as a sheepherder I talked to up in the hills may not have been paying attention?"

"Four or five, last count," Dawson said. "The problem's getting hermits and such outta them headwater canyons before anyone can improve 'em. I'd just go ahead and drown the sons of bitches if they wouldn't move. But they say old Colonel Baxter's a soft-hearted cuss."

Longarm said, "So I heard from a Mormon lady I met up one of them canyons this morning."

"You sure have been all over creation aboard my horse," Dawson replied. He had another drink while Longarm brought him up to date on how he'd come by the black pony to begin with. When he'd finished, and added he'd sure like to know more about what Handsome Luke might have been up to, up here, before he'd helped himself to the saloon keeper's mount, Dawson sighed and said, "Had I known a gent with that much bounty money on his head was anywhere near me he'd have never made it to Vernon."

Longarm sipped some more beer before he observed, mildly, "In all modesty, he was pretty good with a gun, Badger."

The saloon keeper grinned at the gal behind the bar and said, "We know how to shave the odds when wicked gents come in here, don't we, Barbie?"

The bucktoothed Barbie grinned back, a dismal sight, and said, "Chloral hydrate salts sure take a lot of speed out of a man, and it's cheaper than opium as well."

Longarm grimaced and said, "Well, nobody ever accused Handsome Luke of fighting fair. Since he survived a drink or more up this way I'll take your word you didn't know him. Is there a livery here in Shoshone?"

Dawson thought and said, "Yes and no. They'll board your riding stock for you at the Comanche Corral just down the walk. But they don't have mounts to hire out. You may have noticed this town ain't too refined as yet. Do you want to borrow my black pony some more, seeing you know it so well?"

Longarm shook his head and said, "That's mighty Christian of you, Badger. But I don't need a pony for just poking about a settlement so small. I wear old army boots with walking in mind. My question about livery mounts is two-fold. For one thing, I might have to do some more serious riding and you've already missed your personal pony once."

For a man so free with his gun hands, Dawson was a tad shrewder than he looked. He asked what the second reason might be. Longarm hesitated and then, seeing they were being so friendly about his possibles, he confided, "That hired gun I met in Vernon never got here by rail or stage-coach."

Dawson said, "I could have told you that. Everyone here comes in by way of Vernon or the county seat, even farther to the north. It's too far to walk, either way."

Longarm nodded and said, "They didn't know him in Vernon. That means he got this far from further, like you just said. He would have hired, bought, or stolen a mount no closer than the railroad towns of Tooele or Bingham Canyon. By the time he got here he'd have ridden his original mount into the ground. I noticed he didn't treat your black pony all that nice."

Dawson laughed incredulously and said, "Hot damn, that does explain how I lost my swell saddle and pretty good horse so unexpected. But when we noticed him missing, out front, we didn't see no ponies left over."

Longarm drained the last of his free beer, set the schooner back down, and said, "That's why I'd best have a word with 'em at that corral you mentioned. You say she's just down the way?"

They both nodded and Dawson said, "Comanche Corral. Don't ask me why. There ain't never been no Comanche in Utah."

"That's fair," Longarm said. "I've yet to meet a Moor in Dodge but the Alhambra Saloon was built there, anyways."

He ticked the brim of his Stetson at Barbie and ambled outside. He hadn't been giving the canvas roof of the Last Gasp as much credit as it deserved, he saw, when the overhead sun hit him over the head from the cloudless noonday sky. He was so glad old bucktoothed Barbie was minding his frock coat he'd have been willing to do most anything for her but kiss her.

The Comanche Corral consisted of a big empty corral of cedar poles and a stable of more solid frame construction. He knew the owners had to be gentile when he noticed they had Indian views on whitewash. Indians saw no sense in whitewashing, even if most nations hadn't considered white a gloomy spirit color. But Mormons were worse than Tom Sawyer's Aunt Polly when it came to whitewashing frame buildings. Longarm had to sort of go along with the Indians and white folk of the gut-and-git persuasion when he considered whitewashing a jerry-built stable in a one-horse town doomed to an early death or fireproof brick, depending.

It was cooler but stinkier inside. He found a young Mex or breed dozing on some feed bags as the mounts in the stalls beyond were kept more awake by stable flies. The kid opened one eye at the sound of Longarm's heels on the gritty gravel near the entrance and murmured, "Where's your pony, and are we to feed or just water the same 'til you get back?"

Longarm said, "I'm afoot. Before you cloud up and rain all over me I'd best advise you I'm the law, as well."

That made the stable hand sit up straighter. He looked

up sort of big-eyed and protested, "We haven't done anything the law would be after us about."

"I ain't after you," Longarm said. "I'm looking for a mount a man dressed charro might have left here a few days back."

The kid nodded and said, "I recall him with some displeasure. He never came back for his damned roan and I'm too kind of heart to let a pony go hungry and thirsty, unclaimed or not."

"He won't be coming back," Longarm explained. "He left it here and stole another mount, saddle and all, to ride on to Vernon, where he's likely buried by now."

The stable hand rose to his feet, saying, "That accounts for the High Plains roping saddle we got in the tack room, then. My boss says we can sell the pony if nobody comes back for it in thirty days. The saddle ain't worth putting up for auction. We don't get many tie-down ropers out this way and it's sort of beat up to begin with. Come on, I'll show you the roan he stuck us with." So Longarm followed him down between the rows of stalls, with bored and overheated ponies farting at them and swishing their tails at flies. When they got to a roan rump the kid patted it and said, "This is her. If you think she ain't much now, you should have seen the shape she was in when that bastard left her with us. All lathered and brush-cut like he'd ridden her across the sage flats with a war party on his trail. He said he'd pay me extra if I'd curry her back in shape. But he never came back, the son of a bitch."

Longarm moved around to get a better look at the orphan as he said, "Don't be too hard on him. He might have meant it. Then he spotted a better-looking fresh mount, all saddled up and ready to go. So he went. I'm glad I found that much out, even if it may call for me hunting snipe further north. For if Handsome Luke was sent after me from up in the mining country closer to the lake, and he sure acted as if he had been, that means I don't have to look for anyone here in Shoshone who paid him to kill me off."

He slid in between the roan and the side of the stall to pat her neck and get a better look at her as he added, half to himself, "I sure am tired of the way one has to get about out here. How much is your boss asking for this roan, with that roping saddle and bridle thrown in?"

"You'll have to ask him," the kid say. "I just work here. How does forty dollars strike you?"

Longarm said, "Awful. When do you figure your boss will be back?"

The kid shrugged and said, "Maybe around five or six, when the heat dies down. That's a pretty good horse, you know, now that she's been rested and curried some. All her shoes are tight and her teeth make her no older than six or seven."

Longarm smiled thinly and said, "Make that eight or ten and I may believe you. When your boss shows up, make sure you tell him I'm talking about my own money and that I've ridden for the Hash Knife and Captain Goodnight in my time. Then tell him I figure this critter's worth maybe twenty, tops, with that saddle thrown in. I don't have to look at no infernal roper. I ain't out to rope anything and, if the truth be known, I'd as soon have a McClellan if I was shopping for a serious saddle."

"I noticed your army boots and the cavalry tilt to your hat," the kid said. "I'll tell him what you said. I doubt he'll let you get off that easy and, ah, it's sort of far to walk if you're really headed as far as the south shore of the lake."

Longarm didn't argue. He knew he had enough of that ahead of him. He said,"It looks like I'll have to. Meanwhile I may as well see the rest of this here charming community. I keep hearing about a main irrigation ditch around here. How many ditches are we talking about and where's the main one at?"

The young stable hand said, "Head north and you'll come to where it crosses the street out front. They've been talking about bridging it, but maybe they're waiting until they get some water in it. Why would you be looking for a dry ditch at this or any other time, lawman?"

Longarm didn't see it as the kid's business, but since he'd been raised polite he explained, "I'd like a word with the boss of this construction site, as long as I'm here. Since he ain't home, he may be out digging ditches and I'd best start with the most serious one."

They shook on it and Longarm stepped out into the furnacelike glare again. As he passed the Last Gasp a second time he was tempted to go inside and wait out the scorching afternoon more sensibly. But he knew they'd likely expect him to pay for any more suds he inhaled and it wasn't smart to drink a whole afternoon away on the job, whatever infernal job Billy Vail had sent him on.

He found the ditch, crossing the main drag and already torn up a mite from no doubt cussing riders fording the dry dusty bed. He didn't have to cross it. An obvious service road led east across the flats in line with the twenty-foot-wide and four-foot-deep dry watercourse. As he trudged east past the last sunbaked shacks a desert locust rattlesnake buzzed ahead of him on its orange and black imitation butterfly wings, only to land further up the service rut and turn back into a dusty twig again, until he got close enough to make it repeat the fool process. Jackrabbits did the same thing. He'd never figured if jacks and locusts were dumb as hell or liked to tease. The locust did it six or seven times before it finally wised up, or got tired of the game, and landed somewhere out in the dusty sage.

That left Longarm even less to admire as he trudged on down the rutted dusty road. Sagebrush was never all that interesting to look at, even when it was a blossom, sort of mustard yellow. That made him think of that eastern gal he'd met along the Humbolt that time, who'd been confused to see western sage bloomed yellow when she'd been expecting purple. Explaining that herb-garden sage and western sagebrush were two different weeds entire had been a swell way to start a conversation with a pretty gal. Although he'd later suspected, when she damn near busted his back in the Pullman berth, it had been her who'd started that conversation, after all.

He stopped to light a cheroot, telling himself this was no time to think about females in Pullman berths or anywhere else. It was too damned hot to even flirt, and anyone with a lick of sense would have already turned back. For there was nothing out ahead but some black dots flickering in the heat waves under a heat-wavered . . . windmill?

Longarm gripped the cheroot in his teeth and trudged on, muttering, "If they mean to fill this ditch with windmill water, that ain't the way I'd do it. It would take a daisy windmill all day, in a good breeze, to even fill a hundred yards of this old ditch."

Then, as he got closer, he saw that while the windmill rose near a fenced-in homestead claim off the road a piece, the dots along the horizon beyond had no real connection to the house and outbuilding of sun-silvered planking. They'd simply ran the road and ditch past a spread that had no doubt been out here a spell.

As he passed it an old man rocking on the porch waved at him but didn't offer to coffee and cake him. Dwelling this close to a newer service road, the earlier settlers had no doubt by now seen how expensive country manners could get if you overdid 'em."

As he forged on, Longarm saw some of the haze blurring his view of the distant dots was caused by rising dust. As he closed more distance he could see it was a work crew of men and mules, except for one rider off to one side, sitting his bay while the rest of the men and beasts kept ripping open the sage flat at the far end of this canal to nowheres much, so far.

He broke stride when, behind him, he heard the sound of hoofbeats. When he looked back, he spied yet another dot coming his way under a cloud of chalky road dust. It seemed impossible, but while he could see the Cedar

Ranges well enough back that way, he couldn't make out the town at their bases at all. That made it at least three or four miles he'd walked, allowing for the curvature of the earth at ground level. He saw he was now a lot closer to the work crew, so he kept walking, cussing himself for having started in the first damned place. The next time he looked back he didn't see that other rider. He'd likely turned in at that homestead, having sense enough to get a horse before he headed out even that far under such an oppressive heat.

As he got close enough to the work crew to matter he saw they were making sense, after all. The mules were doing most of the work with Mormon plows, with the shovel hands just cleaning up the rough edges after 'em."

The Mormon plow was a mighty slick invention. The Mormon Delta would have been a lot smaller without it. Each team of mules hauled what looked like the wheels of a sulky with the sulky left out. The wheels were only there to hold up that end of the pole the mules were pulling, or maybe pushing was a better way to put it. For at the front end, out ahead of the mules, was a sort of snowpile blade. As the mules pushed forward the blade pushed dirt, sage, and anything else in the way ahead of 'em. Right now they were using three mule teams and three Mormon plows to cut the irrigation ditch further east, in three steps. Shovel hands working to either side, at all three levels, cut the banks at a neater forty-five-degree angle, tossing the spoil out and away as the jasper seated on the saddle pony under a big white hat watched with approval. He saw Longarm coming, nodded, and rode to meet him, calling out, "Enjoy your walk?" in a jovial mint-julep accent.

Longarm called back, "Not if you ain't Colonel Baxter. I'd be U.S. Deputy Custis Long and that's who I'm looking for."

The man under the white hat called back, "You've found him. What can I do for you, sir?" Then he gasped and yelled, "Look out! Behind you!"

So Longarm did, spinning around and dropping to one knee as a bullet parted the air where his shoulder blades had just been.

Since Longarm had drawn his own gun by this time the shabby figure crouched just off the service road in the stirrup-high sage didn't get to fire again before Longarm nailed him just above the heart and sat him down out of sight in the silvery brush. By this time the colonel's spooked horse was crow hopping around in the same sage and the work crew were all yelling at once in confusion. Longarm had no answers, either, so he ran toward the last sight he'd had of the back shooter he'd just shot, his own gun ready for anything left out that way.

But when he found the body sprawled among the sage bushes with its hat over its face, as if some hobo had decided to take a nap just off the road, Longarm could see by the red carnation of fresh gore pinned to the greasy shirtfront that he'd hit the bastard about where he'd planned.

As he hunkered down to toss the hat aside and see what the rascal's pockets had to tell him, Colonel Baxter rode to join them, patting his mount's neck and cussing it sweetly. Longarm said, "Don't ride no closer on a spooky mount, Colonel. You know what the smell of blood does to some of 'em."

The older man dismounted at a safe distance and came the rest of the way afoot, saying, "I know all too well. I rode with old J.E.B. Stuart for The Cause. He was a caution for spilling blood around horses. What just happened here, son?"

Longarm got back to his feet, nudging the cadaver with a toe as he explained, "He must have dismounted somewhere back closer to that homestead and circled after me on foot through the sage."

Baxter said, "I could have told you that. I was staring both your ways when he popped up like a jack-in-the-box to peg that shot at us. My questions are who and why."

"I'm pretty sure I was the who he was out to kill,"

Longarm said. "I'm still working on the why. I saw him earlier today in the Last Gasp Saloon. He was nursing a beer in the corner and I might have known he was listening to my conversation at the bar about another killer called Handsome Luke. I don't reckon he was happy to learn Handsome Luke was no longer with us. Or that I was backtracking the cuss. He's got no I.D. and only a few dollars on him. If you'd like an educated guess, I'd say he's been waiting here for old Handsome Luke to return from an errand in Vernon. I was dumb not to ask if they had any other unclaimed horses at the Comanche Corral, albeit they likely wouldn't have said they had in any case. His sidekick's roan was left there unclaimed because Handsome Luke was in a hurry. This one may have his mount most anywhere, since he was told to wait here. I mean, before he lit out after me just now. He got off somewhere between here and that windmill to the west. If you'd be good enough to scout about some, sir, you'd no doubt find it tethered close enough to save me walking all the way back."

Colonel Baxter said he'd be proud to and added, "We can ride back together. I just came out here to see how my boys are doing and, since it's obvious we've a lot to talk about, what say we do it at my place with the little woman serving us iced tea or stronger?"

"Well," Longarm said, "I sure did want to jaw with you about a mess of mysterious doings, Colonel."

The older man replied, "That's what I just said. Stay here. I'll find that other horse for you."

Chapter 11

Lavinia Baxter didn't serve them ice tea or anything else at first. She ducked into another room to "get properly dressed for unexpected company, you fool." So the colonel did the honors by sitting Longarm down on a built-in sofa as he mixed them something more substantial than iced tea at his built-in bar across the sitting room of his rolling home. The interior struck Longarm as surprisingly roomy. Having most of the furniture built into the walls instead of just shoved against them saved a heap of floor space. There was room for an oriental rug on the floor that looked expensive enough to be real.

By the time the two men were sipping juleps and Longarm had brought his host up to date on his recent misadventures, Lavinia came out to mix herself a stiffer drink. Her notion of proper dress didn't hide much more than her terry cloth robe had. Maybe even less when one considered there couldn't be any undergarments between her Junoesque hide and that summer-weight beige shantung bodice. She hadn't buttoned it all the way up, either.

But for a gal who cussed her man to strangers when he wasn't home, old Lavinia was a gracious enough hostess when he was. Longarm would have preferred her a mite more formal. But her husband didn't seem to mind when she plopped down next to Longarm on the sofa, hip to hip, and commenced to ooh and ah as the colonel told her the young lawman they were entertaining seemed to be getting shot at a lot for a man who didn't know who or what he was supposed to be doing on their side of the Great Divide.

Longarm found her oohs and ahs easier to ignore than the way she kept grinding her hip against his. But since her husband didn't seem to mind, Longarm tried to get off the subject of his own heroism by telling the colonel, "I may be able to find out where that last shabby cuss was staying. I know none of your work crew could I.D. him, so he couldn't have been on your payroll. But, no offense, there's lots of folk drifting in who ain't employed by you."

Baxter nodded and said, "I know all too well. I try to protect my hired hands from the boomers that gather around every barn raising or fence stringing to set up a three-card-monte game or worse. But my company police, as you must know, only have limited authority. Their licenses only give them the right to protect company property or perhaps stop a murder in progress. There's no federal statute against tinhorning, and we are on unincorporated range out here, so far."

Longarm took a sip of julep before he asked, mildly, "Can I take it, then, all the gun hands on your payroll have private licenses from Utah Territory?"

"You can," the older man said. "I've learned the hard way, on other projects, that hiring guns who just drift in can buy a man more trouble than it prevents. I have, let's see, thirty-odd guards riding herd on the hundred square miles we've staked out so far. I can't say I've read the life story of every one of them. But somebody up to Salt Lake

City will have. We haven't taken on one man who didn't have a Utah license, and of course a clean bill of health from the law."

Lavinia said, "Mormon law is sort of fussy, too. The boys my husband's hired, so far, are so clean-living one might call them sissies, guns or no guns."

Longarm didn't ask her to explain. He told the colonel, "In Denver I was told some less sissy looking gents seemed headed this way in numbers. Headed for Vernon, least-ways. I don't see how an obvious gunslick could leave Denver, Colorado, with a Utah hunting license."

Baxter shrugged and said, "I told you every honey pot attracts flies. Maybe some of the local merchants have need of their own toughs. Maybe those more sinister sounding gents went somewhere else from Vernon."

Longarm shook his head and said, "There ain't nothing else within miles, sir. If they were interested in booming mining camps they'd have got off the train way to the north. If they was out to buy up water rights anywhere else, they'd have stayed aboard and got off way south, in the Sevier sink."

The colonel grimaced and said, "You're talking alkali, son. All the land worth irrigating down that way has been claimed and watered by the Mormons by now. I don't re-call us selling any lots to anyone as spooky as you de-scribe. But feel free to peruse our records all you want. Tell 'em at the land office I said it was all right. You'd know better than us if anyone wanted by the law has shown a sudden interest in settling down on his own little celery farm."

Longarm smiled thinly and said, "I doubt anyone wanted by us would do so under his own name. We've been told Frank and Jesse James are holed up like that, further east. To date, neither name has appeared on a land deed or business license. But you may have a point, sir. Out here in the middle of nowhere *would* make a handy place to hide out between jobs, and your lot salesman did quote prices many a man could afford, if he'd just held up a bank in other parts. How soon do you figure you'll have the water running in all them ditches and a big enough crowd out this way for the election of some local law?"

Baxter sighed and said, "We're running behind schedule. We have most of the digging down here on the flats taken care of. But to tell the truth, we need more headwater land up in the hills. There were more early Mormon cliff dwellers than they told us about in Salt Lake City, and some of them are being difficult."

"He means they're holding out for more money," Lavinia said. "If I were a man I'd soon straighten them out. Anyone who doesn't appear on our survey maps is no more than a squatter, and we all know they have no land or water rights."

Her husband looked pained. Longarm told her, gently, "That's not all the way true, ma'am. Whether they got permit from the main temple or not, all the early Mormon settlers out this way were granted certain rights by Washington when we took Deseret, as they called it, away from Mexico back in '48."

She frowned and asked, "How did Mexico get into this and who says Mormons were ever Mexicans?"

Longarm was just as glad to let her husband explain, "They moved out here, to what was then Mexican territory, in order to be free to follow certain odd notions that kept getting them sort of lynched in the then United States. Mexico didn't care. They figured anyone who wasn't a Spanish Catholic was going to hell in any case and meanwhile, any kind of white folk made better citizens of Mexico than antelope and Indians."

She laughed incredulously and said, "Well, I never. I've heard lots of funny things about Mormons, but this is the first time I heard tell they were Mexicans as well."

Longarm explained, "Just nominal Mexican citizens, ma'am. The treaty ending the Mexican War agreed all former Mexican citizens dwelling in the lands ceded to us

140

by Mexico would be granted U.S. citizenship but keep any land, water, or mineral rights they may have held under Mexican law. It's an even bigger pain down in the more crowded border territories. For many a former Mex wound up with a lot more land, free-simple, than he ever could have claimed under the homestead act, or could have afforded to buy outright from the federal land office. But fair is fair, and both sides signed the same treaty. So any old Mormon claims in these parts, dated earlier than 1848, would hold up in court. Trying to run 'em off as squatters would be more expensive than buying or swapping 'em out. The last Mormon War took the U.S. Army to deal with, with every private drawing thirteen whole dollars a month."

The colonel looked concerned and asked, "Do you really think the Avenging Angels would come out of hiding if someone got a local Mormon really upset?"

Longarm nodded and said, "I don't think it. I know it. The Salt Lake temple has disavowed the Danites, official. But a lot of 'em are still around, and any saints they couldn't tell you about in Salt Lake City are likely following the older customs of Deseret."

He brightened and added, "Now *that's* something to look into deeper. Danites riding to secret meetings in the hills could no doubt add up to many a report about mysterious riders acting spooky enough to worry gentiles and even Indians. But you say you've been offering to buy them mountain Mormons out fair and square, sir?"

Baxter nodded and said, "More than fair and, so far, nobody on either side has resorted to threats or even surly comments. I fear my Lavinia, here, is right about them holding out for a better price. But you have my word I haven't done a thing to anyone that might call for Avenging Angels sticking their noses into it."

Longarm said, "I'd best ride about and have a few words with the local saints, anyway. I don't seem to upset 'em as much as even some well-meaning gentiles. I'll try to find out why or if any of 'em are on the prod. You don't have to prod some old hermits with harems much to get 'em acting more upset than sensible. I mind one time, a spell back, I come close to getting killed by Danites over on the Great Salt Desert, and I'd already read the Book of Mormon cover to cover."

"Is it true they think the world is flat?" Lavinia asked.

"The ones I brushed with seemed more upset about our notions of wedded bliss, ma'am. It ain't true young Mormon gals have no say on who they have to marry up with, in the regular Mormon communities. But the old buzzards who'd moved out past the salt flats to live free of even their own temple's rules were sort of hard to get along with."

He turned back to her husband to ask, "Would you have a survey map and a list of them holdouts for me to work with, sir?"

"Not here," Baxter replied. "I can dig all our records out for you over to the land office. Or, if I'm not there, ask whoever is to let you have anything you need."

He dug out his pocket watch, swore silently down at it, and said, "That reminds me, I'm overdue at the south canal. I'd best get going. Where are you staying, Longarm?"

His bemused guest said he didn't know. He'd been planning to ride on until just now. Lavinia said, "He's not going anywhere in this hot sun, dear. If you had any sense *you'd* keep me cool company until it's safe for a mad dog outside. Your men and mules can dig just as fast without you standing over them, you know."

Baxter got to his feet, growling, "A lot you know about men and mules, honey. I got to pop out at 'em every now and again, lest they go to sleep entire."

Longarm started to get up as well. But Baxter told him, "She's right about how hot it figures to get before it gets colder. You stay here and use up some of our ice while I ride down to the diggings in the shade of this Texas hat.

Good hunting, if I don't meet up with you again before you ride over to the hills."

By this time Lavinia had a hand on his thigh to keep him down beside her. So Longarm stayed put as the colonel ducked out. The sass beside him waited until they could both hear his receding hoofbeats before she said, "Alone at last. You know where he's going, don't you?"

"To the south canal?" replied Longarm, hopefully.

"He doesn't like sunstroke any more than you do," she said. "I don't see what he sees in that barmaid at the Last Gasp, but I guess it's like they say. After any man's had steak for a while, he hankers for hash. How do you feel about steak, Custis? You strike me as a man of refined tastes."

He gulped and said, "Nobody would want that buck-toothed gal at the Last Gasp if he had anything at all more reasonable to kiss, Miss Lavinia."

She shrugged and said, "Maybe he doesn't want to kiss her on the lips. They say variety is the spice of life, and he is a man who enjoys life a lot. There was a time he just couldn't leave me alone, but lately, well . . ."

"Speaking of life," said Longarm, as he gently removed her questing hand from his lap, "your husband just saved mine, this very day. I wouldn't want you to think me a sissy. But a man has to draw the line somewhere. So I'd best be on my way, now."

She said, "Pooh, that cold-hearted brute wouldn't give you the time of day without an ulterior motive. You don't owe him anything, Custis, and I'm so hot for you I can taste it!"

He tried to rise again. She wrapped both arms around him and pleaded, "Don't worry about him coming back. If I thought he was coming back I wouldn't feel this desperate. He doesn't *care* if I pleasure myself with another man, darling. Couldn't you tell?"

He kissed back when she kissed him. Any man would have. But as she let him up for air and started popping buttons down the front of her bodice he insisted, "Whether *he* cares or not, *I* have to. I told you the man just saved my life, damn it!"

She shook her head wildly, allowing her hair to come undone, as she said, "If he did it was only because he had a reason. He never does anything without a reason, the big crook."

Longarm allowed her to kiss him some more as he digested that. Adultery, as everyone knew, was a sin as well as foolish. But a lawman, he felt, had certain rights when it came to questioning a lady about crooks. So he relaxed and let her hug him tighter as he asked her, casually, "How come you call him a crook as well as a cheating husband, ma'am?"

By this time she had one tempting breast out, pressed against his shirt, as she told him, "He's always been a crook. How did you think he got so rich? How did you think he got me? The mean thing lies when the truth is in his favor and, like a fool, I listened. Can't you see why he ordered you killed?"

He blinked in sincere surprise and told her, flatly, "That just won't work. Handsome Luke's shabby pal had the drop on me from behind when your man shouted a warning, just in time. So why would he do a thing like that if he'd been the one as hired either?"

"I don't know," she said. "I don't care. Kiss me, you fool."

But he didn't. He hugged her back, friendly enough, but said he was still waiting to hear what her man had done so crooked.

She sat up straighter, unbuttoning her bodice to let it all hang out, bold as brass, as she said, "For God's sake, can't you see this whole irrigation project is a flimflam? Have you seen any *water* in those dry ditches all about?"

"Nope," Longarm said, "I'm paid to be suspicious, too. But I suspect my grasp of numbers may be better than your own. Many a flimflam man has sold many a greenhorn worthless land with a lot of sweet talk about the future. Land looks more expensive when you say a railroad, an irrigation project, or whatever is on its way."

She rose high enough to haul off her dress entirely, and as he saw what both it and that earlier robe had been hiding, he saw he hadn't imagined anything *that* grand. But as she sat back on his lap, naked as a jay and built a lot better, he told her, "It won't work that way. I said I had a head for figures. So I've already added up his payroll, at least one big dam, and all the other work he's done so far. Balanced against the price per acre he's asking for the land he's selling, he'll barely break even if he sells it all. There's just no way he can hope to make a profit before he commences to sell water to all them sudden farm folk."

"Screw the farmers," she said, "or, better yet, screw you know who, you big bashful thing."

He sighed and said, "I ain't bashful, ma'am. I'm just decent. It wouldn't be right to trifle with the woman of a man who just saved my life. So let me up and we'll say no more about it."

She sobbed, "Idiot! He's on his way to another woman this very minute!"

"I'd feel bad about having *her* bare-assed on my knees as well, then. I'm sorry you can't understand the code of a gentleman. But that's all right, you ain't a gentleman, so you don't have to."

Then he gently but firmly shoved her bare rump off his lap to sit it on the sofa and got to his feet, adding, "I do. It's sure been nice talking to you, ma'am. But for both our sakes I'd best get on down the road, now."

She rose to follow him, naked, to the door, saying, "You can't mean this! More than one man has told me right out that I'm good-looking and I've just out and out offered you my all, goddamn you!"

He sighed, ticked his hat brim at her, and swung the dutch door open, saying, "I won't tell if you don't tell, Miss Lavinia."

He could see he hadn't made a mistake when she asked him in a tone of low cunning, "What if I was to say you raped me just now? Wouldn't you just as soon have the game as the name?"

He shook his head and told her, "Nope. Whether others believe me or not, *I* always know the truth about my deeds or misdeeds. But I'm glad you just tried to pull that, Miss Lavinia."

Being a woman, she naturally had to know why. So he smiled coldly down at her naked charms and explained, "I might have felt a lot worse, passing on such delicious albeit forbidden delights, if I didn't know, for sure, you were such a disgusting bitch. Now that I do, I'd as soon kiss that barmaid at the Last Gasp, and that could only take place with her holding a gun to my head."

Chapter 12

Nobody at the Last Gasp Saloon would own up to ever having seen the scrub pony Longarm had inherited from the last owlhoot who'd tried to kill him. Badger Dawson wasn't there, but the bucktoothed Barbie was. Business had picked up as the day wore on and she was serving suds fast enough to sweat, as her customers tried to cool off. Longarm didn't think much of the sweating pony tied up out front, either. So he finished his one beer and led it on down to the Comanche Corral.

The young stable hand asked him if he was going into the horse trading business for himself as he helped Longarm unsaddle and stall the broken-down dun. Longarm replied, "The wages of sin have sure been modest, so far. The only decent profit I've made on this mission was in a card game having nothing to do with horseflesh. When your boss gets back, though, tell him this old dun and its beat-up saddle is his if he wants to make me a deal on that roan that was never his to begin with."

The stable hand allowed the shabby back-shooter's stock and saddle, combined, might be worth fifteen dollars to somebody, but hardly to the Comanche Corral. Longarm said he'd be back later to argue about it.

He walked to the land office tent, partly because he was kind to animals and partly because climbing on and off every few fool minutes in a small settlement wasn't worth it.

Although it was now obvious Lavinia Baxter had made up nasty fibs about the colonel and that ugly barmaid, the colonel wasn't at the land office, either. But the fat salesman didn't put up the argument Longarm was braced for. When told the boss had said it was all right to poke through the files, the lot salesman just excused himself to the Mormon farmer he'd been dickering with, got up from the table, and led Longarm through a flap and into what was either another tent or the back of the same one with a canvas partition screening the doings out back from public eye.

Nothing dirty was going on. A tired, washed-out but sort of pretty little ash blonde was working at a drafting table with a kit of colored pencils and a big survey map thumbtacked to the flat maple surface. The lot salesman introduced her to Longarm as their head and only draftswoman, Peggy Mason, and told her to give the law any information it wanted while he got back to selling lots for IIT.

She didn't argue. She just looked tired as she asked Longarm what she could do for him. Her figure wasn't bad under the limp, damp poplin smock she had clinging to her sweaty hide. But it was too hot to worry about that, even if they'd known one another a lot better. He said, "I ain't sure," and went on to fill her in on the vague rumors that had occasioned his being sent out here to sweat with her in the first place. She seemed sincerely puzzled when he got to mysterious riders and possible Danites.

She went back to filling in a square on the survey map

with a greentipped pencil as she said, "I'm not a Mormon, but I finished high school in Ogden, my father being a railroad man. So I got to know a lot of Mormons, and I can't say I found them difficult to get along with as long as you treat them decent."

He said, "I've found 'em much the same. But the saints you'd have met in a railroad town might qualify as more sophisticated and tolerant than some you might meet out here in almost empty country. Your boss says you've been having trouble getting a few old-time settlers to go along with this irrigation project."

She nodded but said, "Not to the point even an Indian might see fit to go on the warpath." She consulted a bundle of carbon-papered yellow slips tacked to one corner of her drafting table before starting to green in another patch on the map as she went on, "If anyone's been putting pressure on the other side, I'd have to say it was nesters sitting on some water rights. Colonel Baxter is sort of, well, thrifty when it comes to money. But it would cost as much, and be more risky, to run crusty old Mormons off their land than to simply meet their price."

Longarm perked up and asked, "Are you saying nobody has been holding out entire? It's just a question of paying through the nose for some of that high ground?"

She nodded, pointed with her pencil at a patch left blank except for a penciled question mark, and said, "Everyone has his price. You can see the Brown family, here, has a stranglehold on the drainage of this canyon we otherwise have about bought out. Old Man Brown is holding out for three hundred dollars an acre and we're talking about rocky slopes too steep for poison oak to really thrive on."

Longarm moved around to her side to study the contour lines drawn in with lighter brown ink as he agreed, "Three an acre would be a handsome price for Ohio bottomland. I've been up in those hills and, yep, he's so far up we surely are discussing rough sheep range at best. I had breakfast with a Mormon lady dwelling farther down, where cows can just about make it, and she told me right out that she and her man figured to sell out. Old Man Brown must know more about irrigation. I see he's got a spring cut off from your planned reservoir farther down. Has that one been started yet, by the way?"

Peggy shook her head and said, "We can't. There's no sense even starting a reservoir if you don't control the water running into it, see?"

"Yep," he said. "But what if the colonel can't meet their price? Does that mean ruin to his plans down here on the flats?"

She laughed, almost bitterly, and said, "Colonel Baxter can meet their price. He just doesn't want to. I've already assured him we can get by without that side canyon if need be. The dams here, here, and here will back up enough undisputed water to feed the planned canal network well enough. He just feels it would be, well, neater, if we had all the headwaters of The Shoshone all penciled in in blue."

Longarm nodded and said, "I notice you got what I as-sume to be cropland penciled green, land to be flooded penciled blue, and what does yellow mean?"

"Improved rangeland," she said. "The larger but cheaper lots we've sold around the core of green-penciled croplands won't be irrigated by canals. There's a limit to how far you can run irrigation water above ground before it just sinks in. But in doing so it will naturally raise the water table, well out into the sage flats. So homespreads with windmill pumps—"

"Already seen some," Longarm cut in, explaining, "I'm not an expert, but it seems to me you can already drill down to water in these parts. For I've been passing scat-tered windmills all the way up from Vernon. So why would anyone be willing to pay IIT for the privilege? They can claim all the dry range they want off Uncle Sam, free, further out."

She nodded but explained, "They can pay for a lot of

drilling pipe as well. Naturally there's groundwater all along the bases of the Cedar Ranges, but it gets mighty salty further out. I never said we're offering irrigated cattle spreads around the limits of our water project. We're talking about lots for sale at only slightly more than the colonel paid the Interior Department for, ready to use without all that homestead paperwork and well water just eight or ten feet down. An ambitious nester could have fruit trees out back by the time he'd ever prove a homestead act claim. Water apples or pears a few years from your well, 'til they can sink their own roots to the water table, and—"

"Not pears," Longarm cut in. "You plant pears for your heirs. But apples are worth planting out here, over a sensible water table."

He was about to ask a question about the rate irrigation water sank out of sight and regular use in such dry country when a mean-looking individual walked in sort of squatty under a pancaked hat to say, "They told me I might find you here, Longarm. What's the meaning of your high-handed ways on my territory?"

Longarm shot a wary glance down at the two guns the jasper had on, noted he had on a toy badge as well, and replied, "If we are discussing jurisdiction, the workers who put that dead saddle bum aboard a buckboard for me said they'd explain his demise to their company police. I can see by your expression you weren't satisfied in full. Would you be Rex Warner, the old Pinkerton dick that Colonel Baxter said he'd hired to run his private law? If you are, I'd best explain that your boss seemed satisfied I did the right thing. It was him who warned me, just in time, that I was about to catch a pistol ball with my upper spine."

The squat scowler said, "I am Rex Warner, and whether his nibs is satisfied or not, *I* ain't. What gives you the right to kill a man in my jurisdiction and never say a word about it to *me?*"

The gal, Peggy, must have felt sort of awkward about their heated conversation in such an overheated tent. For she left with a mumble about getting some water. That left Longarm free to say, "I was meaning to pay a courtesy call on you before I rode on. I just can't be everywhere at once and this call was more important."

The construction company law growled, "The hell you say. You killed a man on my beat and never even saw fit to tell me who the hell he was. You ain't riding nowhere until you explain your murderous conduct to my satisfaction and, as for how important it might be to jaw with Peggy Mason, she's just a dumb pencil pusher who don't know shit and don't put out."

Longarm stepped well clear of the drafting table, faced the older but obviously dumber man more squarely, and said, "I had a dog named Rex, once. Never could get him house-trained. You must not have been brung up fit for human company, neither. Fortunate for you, the lady you just mean-mouthed in my presence wasn't in my presence. So don't do it again and we'll say no more about it."

Warner almost snarled, "Goddamn it, I'm not worried about your love life, Longarm. It's your own manner with a six-gun I'm so upset about."

"That dog chased wagon wheels for no good reason, too, as I look back on it," Longarm said. "One of my elders finally had to lead him off somewhere and get rid of him. What good was a hound who shit on the rug and wouldn't hunt sensible?"

Warner gasped and demanded to know if Longarm was threatening him. So Longarm smiled thinly and said, "Nope. Just trying to get you to stop barking at wagon wheels, Rex. To begin with, I shot that back shooter in *my* jurisdiction. Until this territory gets its own incorporated government it's part of the federal range of Utah Territory. Didn't they teach you in the Pinks that any *real* lawman, even a town constable of an incorporated township, has jurisdiction over that chunk of scrap metal we allow you to wear as a courtesy?"

Warner almost roared, "See here, I'll have you know

I'm licensed as a lawman by the territorial government in Salt Lake City!"

Longarm shrugged and said, "I just told you it was a courtesy. Now I'd best tell you that if you shit with me I can rip that toy badge off you with one wire to the Utah License Bureau. If you bothered to read the small print on the back, you'd already know how limited your powers are and that you're not allowed to fuss with real lawmen. So don't fuss with me no more."

Rex Warner began to puff up like an old frog who'd just been challenged for its hitherto private lily pad and then, since he wasn't as much a moron as a natural bully, he deflated and sort of whined, "Nobody said anything about arresting a U.S. deputy for killing a suspect in front of witnesses, damn it. But it was rude as hell to leave us stuck with a body in this heat without even telling us who it *belonged* to."

Longarm could meet anybody halfway. So he smiled nicer and explained, "I don't know who he was. He was packing no I.D. and I can't recall his unshaven face from any recent Wanted fliers. If you'll settle for a guess, I suspect he was riding with a more established killer called Handsome Luke Harding. I got to shoot it out with him down Vernon way the other night. The law there was not only real but less rude. So guess who got to put in for the bounty?"

Rex Warner began to sound more reasonable indeed as he said, "I've heard of Handsome Luke. He was a mean son of a bitch. Is it your opinion that shabby stranger we got boxed in salt and tanbark over to my lockup could be posted as well?"

Longarm said. "I doubt he could have been a traveling parson Harding picked up in his travels for companionship. He might have just been an ambitious saddle bum, upset with me because I gunned his mentor just as he was learning the ropes. *His* attempt on me was sort of dumb. To learn how long he'd been backing the play of a better-known killer, we'd start by sending out an all-points, if you had a telegraph office in this infernal camp."

Rex Warner allowed, morosely, that the nearest Western Union office was down south in Vernon. Longarm said, "You might want to send a rider down yonder to wire about for you, then. I ain't half as worried about who he *was* as who he was *working* for. Nobody at the saloon or corral could even I.D. his pony. So I'll take your word he wasn't working for your outfit. He must have been staying somewhere in camp for at least a few nights, though. Your turn, Rex."

The squatty company dick thought hard and then said, "Shacked up with some camp follower, most likely. We try to discourage that sort of shit. But any construction payroll draws more camp followers than a dead horse draws flies. We got disgusting gals of ever' age and price selling their services in ever'thing from red river carts and tar-paper shacks to real frame houses trucked in. We can start with the regular whorehouses, if you like."

Longarm shook his head and said, "I don't like that at all, Rex. Time could be of the essence and, even if you find some gal with such poor taste, she'd likely lie about it. It's pure hell to get a whore to admit aiding and abetting a killer, and by now the whole settlement knows how unpleasant the cuss was."

"I still mean to ask around," Warner said. "Where will you be in the meantime?"

Longarm looked around and said, "I don't know, for sure. I had some more questions to ask that Miss Peggy. But she sure takes her time drinking water."

Rex Warner looked about, too, as if to make sure he couldn't be overheard, before he confided, "You won't get anything out of her. I know you said not to mean-mouth her. But seeing we're on the same side about any money posted on that rascal you contributed to us, she's said to be the colonel's private stock."

Longarm raised an eyebrow to reply, "Do tell? Are we

talking known fact or the sort of talk a pretty gal is inclined to draw just by saying no a few times?"

"I've never caught her with the boss bare-assed," Warner said, "if that's what you mean. But it's an established fact he's been cheating on his wife with *some* gal, hereabouts, and I just told you most of the local talent was sort of trail-worn and too cheap for the likes of a man who orders his drinks by brand name."

"I suspect I know where that gossip started," Longarm said. "I was told it was another gal I know for a fact it can't be. I'd like you to consider, and pass around, that while cheating wives tend to suspect the local preacher's wife, it's been my experience that a rich man's mistress seldom puts in a hard day's work at less agreeable chores. A gal that good-looking could doubtless make as much or more loafing on a sofa with a box of chocolate and a maid doing her hair and spraying her with perfume."

Rex Warner grimaced and said, "That sounds like the old man's wife, save for the maid they don't have."

Longarm said, "Maybe having to do her own hair out here is what upsets her disposition. You can see the colonel ain't here with his pants down, and when I come in, just now, Miss Peggy was perched on that hard stool, sweating like a mule, and if she's drawing two bits an hour for all that neat drafting, it ain't enough. So I don't want nobody mean-mouthing her no more, hear?"

Rex Warner agreed, they shook on it, and Longarm left to see what anyone else might have to tell him. As he ducked out into the hot sun, he heard the heated roar of a six-gun. So he started running with his own gun out.

Chapter 13

The source of the gunplay was easy enough to locate. A considerable crowd had gathered around the entrance of the Last Gasp. Longarm didn't have to bull his way through. Rex Warner had kept up with him, despite having shorter legs and a heavier gun rig. So Longarm just had to follow as the bossy company dick cussed and pistol-whipped his way inside.

It was almost as crowded, and only a little cooler, where Badger Dawson lay facedown near the bar. Bucktoothed Barbie had either vaulted the bar or run around one end. For she was kneeling beside the saloon keeper, crying fit to bust as she tried to shake him awake by the back of his bloody vest. Longarm shoved a construction hand out of the way to hunker down by the sobbing barmaid, saying, "Leave go his duds, Miss Barbie. That could hurt him if he's still alive and can't do much for him if he ain't."

Then he felt the side of the downed man's throat,

sighed, and announced, "He's gone. Did anyone in here see who did it?"

The old swamper came forward to say, "I did and I didn't. The boss had just stepped in when somebody opened up on him from out front."

A Mormon nester closer to the door called out, "He's right. I make it three bullet holes in this one swinging door."

But bucktoothed Barbie sobbed, "That's left over from a drunk Badger throwed out a week ago. The son of a bitch who gunned him today held one bat-wing open and fired low and dirty with his other hand."

Rex Warner said, "Don't keep us in suspenders, girl. Who did you see there or, if you didn't know him, what did he *look* like?"

The ugly tear-streaked barmaid answered, "I can't say. He was just a man, dark against the sun. I never looked up from the beer I was pouring until he was already firing and poor Badger, here, was going down. I can't be sure. I wasn't paying attention, but I think the two of them were talking, out front, just before it happened. I know Badger was talking to somebody, because I wasn't surprised when he came in, muttering something under his breath. Then it got all noisy and gunsmokey in here and, oh, Lord, he *can't* be dead. He's the best boss I ever had and I ain't been paid yet this week!"

A portly gent in a stuffy dark suit hunkered down as well to hand the distraught barmaid his card as he told her, "Don't you worry your pretty head about that, Miss Barbie. I'll see you get paid off the books or my time at Harvard Law was surely wasted."

Someone back in the crowd chimed in, "I was across the street at the feed store when the shots rung out. I didn't see nobody running off, though."

Longarm stared soberly at Warner, who nodded and said, "Yeah, that's the way a professional would have done

157

her. It takes nerve, but nobody recalls a man just walking, when the whole world is acting excited. You reckon Handsome Luke could have left more'n one sidekick, here, to wait for him?"

Longarm shook his head and said, "I doubt it. Harding and his bunch were sent after me for whatever reason. There's no telegraph office here. Anyone ordered to kill both me and this poor gent would have got to him first, not later. Would anyone here be able to say whether Badger had any local enemies?"

There was a murmured chorus of denial. Bucktoothed Barbie said, "He was a good old boy. Ask anyone. He may have had a temper. But he's yet to really hurt anybody here in Shoshone."

Another local said, "That's right. He sold liquor at a fair price and gave water and pretzels away free. Nobody with a lick of sense had call to back shoot old Badger."

Longarm took hold of the bucktoothed barmaid's arm and got her to rise with him, murmuring, "It's time to talk private, ma'am." So she went with him into the back room down at the end of the bar and as soon as they were alone, he asked her, "How did Badger Dawson get his name, Miss Barbie?"

She looked blank, then asked, "How should I know? He had it when I came to work for him, let's see, six months or more ago. What's wrong with being called Badger? I thought it went with his sort of growly nature."

"It goes with an old flimflam called the badger game, as well," Longarm said. "I don't suppose you've ever heard of it?"

She went on looking blank. So he told her, "The way the setup works is the badger, or sucker, is lured into bed by a pretty gal for what he expects to be some free slap-and-tickle. Only, before it gets that pleasant, another gent busts in on them to announce he's caught the badger in bed with his very own wife and that now he's going to call the law or at least divorce her a heap, naming the badger as her lover and seeing his name winds up on the front page of the local paper. Guess what comes next."

The barmaid smiled wanly and said, "Give me *some* credit for having been around and learning human nature. Naturally the poor badger would rather pay off the outraged husband than have his own wife read about him in the morning papers, and naturally the other two of them was in on it from the beginning."

He nodded, curtly, and said, "A man given to working the old badger game would be more likely to be called Badger than a man who'd fallen for it. Before you answer my next question, I'd best assure you such pretty con games ain't federal and that I'm only out to find out why your boss wound up so dead, lest it be *me* the next time."

Bucktoothed Barbie seemed sincerely puzzled as she assured him, "He never pulled a stunt like that with me, although I sure thank you for the compliment. Before you ask, I was the only gal on his payroll."

"Were you sleeping with him as well?" Longarm asked, flatly.

She laughed incredulously and said, "Lord love you for the flattering gent you are. Do you think I'd be dumb enough to pump suds all day and then offer my all to a man who only let me have four bits a day and tips? I know I ain't all that pretty, but I ain't stupid, neither. Any man who wants to sleep with *this* girl had best offer her a ring or at least toss some mighty nice grit in her gilded cage."

Longarm had to laugh at the picture of her reclining bare and ugly on red velvet, stuffed with chocolates. He conceded, "Well, like you said, he was as growly as a badger and that way works as well as a nickname. Maybe he simply growled at the wrong gent. He almost got in a fight with me that time and I'm noted for my sweet disposition."

"They did have words before Badger got shot down like a dog," she said. "But don't that mean at least one gent

159

meaner and more dangerous than you has to be wandering about, outside?"

Longarm said, starkly, "He could be inside, looking innocent, if he's really a professional. I'm sure starting to hate this mission. There has to be some point to it. For it's been noisy as hell since I got off my train from Denver. I'll be damned if I can figure out what's going on or, for that matter, what *could* be going on!"

Chapter 14

Longarm bought his supper off an old lady who must have been more Paiute than Mex, since her beanery served chili con carne too bland for a Swede to endure. Her coffee was good and strong, though, and her apple pie wasn't bad. So he was enjoying a second slice when Miss Peggy Mason from the land office came in and sat down beside him. She'd swapped her smock for a thin print summer dress. Neither of them were sweating as bad, now that the sun was setting over behind the Cedar Ranges. He said, "Evening, ma'am. I didn't know you ate here, too."

"I've never been here before," she said. "I've been looking all over for you, Custis."

He signaled the old lady behind the counter to fetch another cup of coffee, at least, and told the tired-looking blonde, "I been looking all over, too. Didn't even find another horse to go with that stranger who gunned Badger Dawson, earlier."

She asked, "How do you know it was a stranger?"

"That's what I just said. It seems to be just one of them things that happen to a man with a peppery temper and the habit of selling red-eye to outdoor types. Murder pure and simple ain't a federal crime. So I'm leaving the case to old Rex Warner. Him and me is pals, now."

She looked away as she murmured, "I was listening. Both your voices were clear enough, through the canvas, as I stood on the shady side."

He washed down some pie with black coffee before he told her, mildly, "Folk who eavesdrop tend to hear things they might not feel too pleased about, Miss Peggy. I hope you stayed there long enough to hear old Rex agree the gossip about you was doubtless just talk."

She ignored her own coffee as she said, "It's not the first time I've heard such gossip about me and the colonel. You were so right and so, well, understanding, when you said I didn't seem a girl who'd have to put up with anything like that just to hold a job. I wish he paid me as much as you seem to think I'm worth, though. I'm sure I could do better, almost anywhere, and it would have to be cooler."

He nodded and said, "I never advise nobody to get married, go to war, or quit their job. But since you brung it up, I've seen want ads for draftsmen in the *Denver Post*, offering a dollar a day or more."

"I'm a woman," she said. "But I'm surely worth as much as I've been getting *here*, and I wouldn't have to put up with all that guff about whether I put out, as Rex phrased it so delicately."

He nodded and said, "Don't let me stop you. I don't see much future for you here, once they sell off the last of them lots you get to color in."

"I felt sure I could count on a man with so much understanding. When are we leaving?"

He almost choked, managed not to, but still had to inhale more coffee before he replied, "I didn't know we were. It's true I mean to ride on, once it cools off some. But to tell the truth I'd yet to come up with a sensible direction. There's nothing up Skull Valley way, bothering the Indians. I have it on good authority from at least two ladies I met over in the hills that nobody has tried to scare either. You told me this afternoon that I'd be wasting my time jawing with the few hill settlers I missed coming in, if they ain't at war with IIT or vice versa. I've about reached the point where a struck lawman commences to wire home and all over for suggestions."

She said, "I surmised you might be heading back to Vernon. I don't think I'd feel safe, alone, on the sage flats. I was hoping you'd let me ride down there with you."

He started to say no. Then he wondered why in thunder a man would want to ride that far, alone, when he could enjoy at least the conversation of a pretty lady. So he asked if she had her own mount and when she confided she had a dear little pony he told her, "Make sure you change into something more fit for the trail and pack some grub along with your frillies. Meet me at the Comanche Corral just after sundown and if I have a mount of my own worked out, we'll see."

She leaped up with a delighted little laugh, gave him a peck on the cheek, and ran off to get packed. He drank the coffee from her untasted cup, left an extra nickel on the counter, and told the lady on the far side, "We're just friends, ma'am."

But the old woman grinned dirty and said, "Ay, muchacho, I wish I could find a friend like you. That one is crazy for your moustache, no?"

He rose, laughing, to reply, "Let's just call her impulsive," and went out to head for the corral.

Before he could get there Colonel Baxter, on foot as well, cut him off to say, "I've been looking for you, Longarm. Do you think that shoot-out at the Last Gasp could have anything to do with the whatever you were sent out here to investigate?"

"I doubt it," Longarm said. "Sometimes it feels that way, but everyone who gets shot in this country might not be connected to my own troubles. It wasn't a shoot-out, by the way. The man who murdered Badger Dawson was a shit-eating yellow dog. Old Badger would have been glad to have a fair shoot-out with him. They'd been talking, heated, before Badger turned away and caught three rounds with his back."

Baxter shrugged and said, "I doubt if either was on my payroll. My draftswoman, Peggy Mason, tells me you were asking about a few holdouts I've been trying to buy out. She seemed sort of uneasy, as well. Just what did you question her about?"

Longarm said, "Nothing that should have upset her. To tell the truth, she said you've been dealing on the up and up with them and that they've just been holding out for more money. Could she be wrong, sir?"

Colonel Baxter looked indignant and snapped, "You can ask 'em if anyone from IIT has been threatening 'em in any damned way, and if anyone says we have he's a damned liar!"

Before Longarm could explain he wasn't up to wasting any more time in the nearby hills, the squatty Rex Warner hailed them from the shade of the walk across the way and came to join them, saying, "We got a name to go with that shabby cuss you shot, earlier, Longarm. Some of the boys changing shifts was naturally curious enough to have a look-see, and more than one recalled the ugly face from Virginia City. They say he answered to the handle of Omaha Orwell when he was working as a hard-rock mining man over that way. He got fired partly for drinking on the job and mostly for highgrading. Miners ain't supposed to take their work home with 'em after hours. They say that after he got run out of Virginia City he was seen up around Carson City, standing trial for horse theft. He got off. It happens that way, sometimes. I couldn't find nobody who recalled him, earlier, around this here part of the world."

Longarm nodded and said, "He wouldn't have been here long enough to leave a lasting impression if he was riding with Handsome Luke Harding. I'll put some feelers out on him by wire once I get to Vernon."

They both looked surprised. Colonel Baxter said, "I didn't know you were heading all the way back to Vernon. Does that mean you've given up?"

"I ain't allowed to give up," Longarm said. "But I've already shot the only cuss in Shoshone who might have told me who him and Handsome Luke were working for. I've found in the past that once the trail across the ground looks cold it's time to start trailing by telegram. I got pals up at the Salt Lake temple as well as the territorial governor's office. The saints are a caution for keeping records. They can even tell you where your ancestors come from in the old countries if they got you on their rolls as a convert. So I can likely find out more about the saints squatting in the nearby hills from old temple records than they might want to tell a gentile in the flesh. Now that I know the last cuss who tried to kill me once stood trial in Carson City, I ought to be able to find out all sorts of things about him and his associates as well. You done good, Rex. I'm sorry I may have hinted you needed housebreaking."

They all shook on it and Longarm left them to trudge on to the Comanche Corral as his purple shadow preceded him in the sunlit dust. When he got there, he found the owner jawing with the young stable hand. The man one really had to see about horse dealing was a crusty old cuss with a Texas twang and confirmed opinions about horses. He said he wouldn't take the beat-up old dun as a gift, let alone partial payment for the roan Longarm wanted, and added, "You're getting a bargain at four bits with saddle and bridle throwed in."

Longarm said, "I don't need to buy saddle and bridle, since you agree you've no claim on the dun that back shooter left me. I'll buy a hack and packsaddle off you, though. I figure to ride the roan and let the dun carry my possibles."

The old-timer spat and said, "Since I've seen all the saddles we're discussing, I feel obliged to warn you the rig on that dun has a cracked tree repaired by haywire and its bridle wasn't in much better shape."

Longarm said, "I noticed. I only mean to ride as far as the telegraph office in Vernon and maybe on to the rail depot a few miles further, not to donate nothing to a museum. So let's talk about basic transportation. I'll give you two bits for that roan if you throw in any board I may owe you on one or both critters."

"Twenty-five dollars is outrageous!" gasped the old Texan.

I know," Longarm said, "but I'm in a hurry." So the sly old-timer laughed despite himself and they shook on it.

The three of them had just cinched a pine packer to the dun and the late Omaha Orwell's battered stock saddle to the roan out front, when Miss Peggy Mason showed up aboard her dear little pony, a barrel-headed blue scrub standing a good fifteen hands high and trying to live down some plow horse on its family tree. The gal was wearing a split skirt but still sitting the brute side-saddle. She'd loaded what looked like two laundry bags, chock full, behind her. When Longarm got done laughing he said, "Well, I wasn't planning on riding at a dead run after dark to begin with. Why don't you wait for me here while I cut back to the Last Gasp Saloon and pick up my own possibles, ma'am?"

She said she'd come along. But he told her she was wrong, explaining, "It ain't no place for a lady, even by broad day, and we'll get started sooner if I don't have to bust no jaws for making unseemly remarks, Miss Peggy. I won't be long. But you and your dear little pony might start out more frisky if you get down and water him some as you rests your, ah, fundamentals."

Not waiting to watch her do so, Longarm mounted the roan and led the dun the short distance back to the saloon. He was glad he hadn't let the pretty little gal tag along when he saw how crowded and noisy the Last Gasp could get at this hour.

He bulled through the construction workers and local nesters to the bar, to ask bucktoothed Barbie for the gear he'd left to her tender mercies. She told him to damn it hold his horses while she filled an order. So he did, leaning against the mahogany as a much better looking gal across the way sang "Up In A Balloon" while perched up on top of the piano. As the uglier barmaid got his pack and water bags atop the fake mahogany for him he told her, "I had a Winchester with this stuff, Miss Barbie."

She told him, "I know. Poor Badger took it somewhere for safekeeping. I don't know where."

He started to argue, considered what he'd paid for Handsome Luke's Winchester to begin with, and said, "Never mind. I'm in a hurry. Who's running this place, now, and didn't you tell me before that you were the only gal working here?"

Bucktoothed Barbie grimaced at the prettier gal singing for all the attention across the way and said, "The answer to both your questions is there, singing about balloons off-key. Badger would have a fit about it if he was still alive. But he ain't. So whether they was married up lawsome or whether she was just his private stock, she says she owns the place now, and that she can go on and sing all she wants on her own piano. Her name is Mary Jo. Do you want me to fetch her over when she gets done howling?"

Longarm started to nod. Then he shook his head and said, "I have another lady waiting to go night riding. I reckon it stands to reason old Badger had a wife or what-

167

ever, since you say he was able to act decent to you, Miss Barbie. Have you worked out your back wages with the, ah, new owner?"

The barmaid nodded grudgingly, and said, "I got no complaints, if only she'd shut up or at least stop flirting so bold with her man barely gone stiff tonight."

Longarm agreed some widows got merry sooner than others and then, since that wasn't a federal offense, he bade the ugly but more respectable barmaid adios and hauled his possibles out to pack on the dun.

A few minutes later he and Miss Peggy Mason were out of camp and riding across the sage flats as a big orange moon rose, full, to shed some light on the subject.

The gal riding sidesaddle to his right looked about in some confusion to announce, "We don't seem to be following any trail, Custis."

"You just noticed? I know where we are, and I've two reasons not to take the regular trail south. For one thing, now that I know the lay of the land better, I'd as soon cut over to the Cherry Creek trail and follow that on in to Vernon. There's water and some tree shade once the sun catches us out here again. I ain't got enough water in them bags for you, me, and three ponies unless we ration it."

She asked what the other reason might be. He shot her a look of admiration and said, "Don't worry your pretty little head about it. I may be overcautious. But without a rifle to call my own, I like to ride where there's more cover and, if possible, I like to make sure nobody is on my trail."

She looked worried, anyway, as she asked, "Do you think someone could be following us?"

He replied, "Someone *could* be doing most anything. We both let more than one person know we were headed down to Vernon. On the other hand, anyone really interested ought to assume we're taking the usual more direct route. So forget about it. If I took it all that serious I'd

168

be riding with a Winchester instead of a gal at the moment."

They didn't ride due east. That would have been too far out of their way. With the moon and stars to steer by, Longarm chose to veer across the sage flats at a thirty-degree angle from the west trail, figuring to hit the east trail along the water and willows any time before sunrise. When she pestered him some more on that point he explained, "We'll make such time as we can by the cooler light of that moon up yonder. There's no way we're going to make her all the way to Vernon this side of some considerable sunlight, even if we abuse our mounts. So it's best to take it easy, rest 'em once an hour or so, and maybe make camp among the cotton-woods and willows when we get to 'em."

She said, softly, "Oh, I didn't foresee we might have to camp out before we got to the railroad."

"That's doubtless why you chose such a fast as well as dear little pony, then," he said. "Are you saying you don't have a bedroll to call your own amid all that luggage be-hind you?"

She shook her head and said, "Just my personal things. Mostly clothing. The place I was boarding at, back there, provided all the bed linens and such I needed. Why do you ask?"

He muttered, "Never mind. We've been riding about an hour now. We're on a patch of cheat as well. Let's get down and rest the brutes a spell."

They dismounted to stretch their legs as the three ponies got to nibble almost useless but maybe entertaining straw. She said something about washing her hands and wandered off into the darkness for a spell. Longarm got out a cheroot and started to light it. But he didn't. He was just chewing the unlit smoke for practice when the gal rejoined him, looking off into the distance as she murmured, "Did you hear something just now, over that way?"

"I wasn't sure," he said. "But the two of us might make

it unanimous. I made it out as the jingle of a night bird or the chirping of a chain harness lead. What did it sound like to you?"

"A jingle," she said. "Or, then again, maybe a bird. Do you think someone could be following us, Custis?"

He cocked his head and didn't answer right away. When he did he said, "If anyone was, they ain't moving right now. We ain't so far from that regular trail, and sounds carry far across flat ground at night. It could have been a wagon wheel on a rocky patch, a lot farther than one could hear less noisy jingles. But just for the hell of it, let's lead our brutes afoot a spell, slow and sneaky, due east. Nobody taking a shortcut ought to be changing directions, see?"

She did. She was a smart old gal for a pencil pusher who tried to ride cross-country with neither bedding nor a gun to call her own. After they'd moved on a spell without hearing any more suspicious noises, Longarm dug out his watch chain and handed it to her, saying, "Here, you can pack this just in case you have any sudden reasons to check the time."

She didn't answer until she'd had time to examine his gift. Then she said, "I see there's a watch at one end and a little *gun* at the other, Custis."

"I know. I'll want 'em both back, later. Have you ever fired a derringer? A small gun, loaded so ferocious, kicks pretty good. So try to make your first shot count if you have to fire it at all."

She bundled it all up to put down the front of her bodice as she told him, "I don't think I could hit the side of a barn if I was standing inside it. But I have fired my father's old pepperbox a few times."

He almost growled, "I hope you treated it with more respect. That derringer's on safety, thank God. If you have to draw, and can, from under your fool frilly top, push down with your thumb on the bitty lever you'll feel there as you haul back on the exposed trigger. With any luck, the safety will snap back on as the first shot bucks it out of your fist."

She grimaced and said, "Oh, come on, my daddy's pepperbox was a .36 and I never dropped it once. It's just that I couldn't *hit* anything with it, like I told you. Why are you talking so scary about guns, Custis? Surely you can protect me with that big .44 of your own, can't you?"

He said, "Not if I'm back shot. So far, none of the gents I've met around here seem to *want* to fight it out fair. Let's mount up again and put some distance between our backs and them."

Chapter 15

By the time they'd ridden through the night, twenty miles or more, Longarm knew the life story of Miss Peggy Mason more than anyone but a book writer needed to. Her tale wouldn't have made much of a book even if he had been in that line of work, although, as travelers on many a train had noticed in the past, there was nothing like jawing with a total stranger, killing time, when it came to spilling things one might hesitate to spill to the neighbors back home. As Longarm had learned, after traipsing off to art school and Lord knows where, Peggy Mason had led a life her kith and kin no doubt felt scandalous, although much of it seemed downright tedious to Longarm. She'd started out to be a regular artist and had to settle for draftsmanship, or draftswomanship, upon learning how easy it was for plain old artists of either sex to starve to death. He questioned her some about the charts she'd been at for IIT, but he soon learned that if she'd found 'em all that interesting she'd have stayed back there, coloring in lots as they were sold, watered or whatever. She kept drifting back to her wanderings and all the men who'd tried to take advantage of her until Longarm began to feel he had to be the only white man west of the Big Muddy who hadn't tried to take advantage of her. It made him feel a mite left out and warned him, for he'd heard her sad story before, that there was no sense getting his hopes up. He'd never figured out why, but it was the gals who talked a lot about *ex*-lovers who didn't seem to want to take on any *new* ones. He'd always had better luck with the shy-talking ones.

But since he couldn't get her off the subject, he asked her whether any of the gents she'd worked for, recently, had messed with her or tried to. From the way she dismissed all the office help back there, he could see why she was in such a hurry to go somewhere else.

He said, "I heard another tale from the overheated and maybe overimaginative Lavinia Baxter. According to her, your boss was a horny old rascal. She had him messing on the side with a barmaid I know I wouldn't, and aside from that, I don't see how he could have. Did you know a gal back there called Mary Jo?"

Peggy said she didn't, and asked who they were talking about as well as why. He said, "Let's veer a mite south. We seem to be alone out here, after all. I didn't know of her being in Shoshone neither, until just as we were leaving. Like old Lavinia, she may have spent a lot of time out of the hot sun to guard her pale complexion. She was the woman of the late Badger Dawson, or so one witness says. It just occurred to me that a jealous wife who wasn't allowed to belly up to the bar with the boys in a he-man saloon might put two and two together to get a mess of buck teeth."

Peggy laughed and said, "I'm sure there must be a point to what you just said, but I just can't fathom it."

He shrugged and said, "I'm just mulling over gossip that ain't federal even if there's anything to it. I can't see anyone ordering a deputy murdered just to keep his wife in the dark about his messing around. Let's get back to what *else* someone could be trying to hide in these parts. Working in that land office, you'd have noticed if your boss had other worries on his mind, right?"

She grimaced and asked, "How many times do you mean to ask me that, Custis? There simply hasn't been any of that mysterious riding you were sent to look into."

He sighed and said, "I noticed. My own boss must have beed fed a bum steer. I mean to tell him so, by wire, once we get to the Western Union in Vernon."

She rode on a ways in silence before she asked him, sort of thoughtfully, "Will you be riding on with me as far as the rails at Lofgreen?"

"I doubt it. I'd like to ride all the way back up to Ogden with you aboard that train. But my boss may have further instructions for me at Vernon. In any case, I can't leave until I get some answers to a mess of questions I'll be sending out from there. There has to be *some* point to this mission, and I'll catch pure hell if I come home empty-handed."

For some reason that lapsed her into a thoughtful, almost sullen silence. So, while the night was almost shot, the rest of it seemed longer until, just before dawn, they spotted trees above the moonlit sage ahead and he told her with a chuckle, "There you go. We've made her to Cherry Creek."

But when they busted through the cottonwoods and willows they found the watercourse bone dry and he had to say, "Well, at least there's shade and we got the water bags."

She yawned and said, "Thank God, I'm really tired, and our poor ponies must feel worse. Where do you think we ought to pitch our camp, Custis?"

Longarm started to say something dumb. Then he decided, "Well, it might be best to bed down among these here willows during the heat of the day and push on later, seeing as there's no hurry."

So one thing led to another until, by the time the sun was up, the brutes were tethered in one place, watered and browsing dusty but juicy cottonwood leaves, and Longarm and the gal were getting to know one another better on his spread-out bedding in a clump of willow, though they were atop the covers, still dressed.

The first time he kissed her she giggled and told him he was fresh. But when he said he was sorry and stopped, she told him anyone from back home who heard she'd bedded down with a good-looking man was never going to believe it had been platonic in any case. So he told him not to tell them about it back home and when he kissed her again she didn't resist as he proceeded to undress her in the dappled shade. But, being a woman, she felt obliged to tell him, "For heavens sake, it's broad daylight and you said there's a trail following this dry creek bed!"

"It can't be helped, little darling," he said. "There's no way to make love more formal to a gal wearing an infernal split skirt and, even if there was, there's green grass all around and the trail's on the far side. I picked this side with that in mind."

She giggled and said she might have expected such a sneaky move from him. But as he shoved his gun rig among the roots of a willow and got to work on his own buttons she covered her bare breasts with her arms and demanded, "Pull the covers over us, at least. I'll just die if anyone comes along to catch us like this!"

He assured her they'd hear anyone using the trail on the far side of a considerable wash in plenty of time to do that and added, "Nobody will ask what we're doing here if we don't tell 'em. It's natural to bed down in shade after sunrise in these parts." Then he got his pants out of the way and got to treating her natural indeed as she moaned and groaned and made him promise to respect her when the sun went down.

He said he would, and once she got over her first shyness there was a lot to be said for daylight loving, provided there was any shade at all and both parties were built good-looking. They took a breather and shared a smoke before she confided she wanted to be abused some more. So they were going at it hot and heavy again when the first shot rang out.

It was a good thing the rifle round that whizzed across Longarm's bounding bare buttocks did so as he was going down instead of up. For, even so, it stung him a heap and left her gasping with an inward thrust she'd long remember. Then he'd rolled off, got his gun out, and hissed, "Stay flat as you can. If that shot came from where I hope it came from, your pretty little head is just below the level he can get at!"

Then another rifle ball tore a sliver of willow bark off, just above them, and he muttered, "See what I mean? Stay put, I'll try to circle the son of a bitch!"

"In your birthday suit?" she sobbed, as he rolled away from her, as flat as he could manage in the grass of their willow grove. He made it to the far side of some brush rising to meet the weeping branches from overhead and, as he raised both his head and .44-40 for a look-see, the first thing he saw was a pony tethered far out among the sage, past rifle range. That put the man who'd just spanked his bare ass with a bullet closer. Longarm didn't spot him until Peggy cried out, "Custis, where are you? I'm scared!" and the bastard fired at her, from where he was hunkered in the sage.

Longarm didn't fire at the blue haze of the rifle. It was a mite far for a pistol ball, even if he'd been able to locate the rascal better. So Longarm started crawling like a sidewinder on his bare belly. Then Peggy must have gotten to the derringer he'd lent her. For she fired it, blind, and though she didn't hit their unseen attacker, or even come near him, the gutless wonder suddenly broke cover to streak for his own mount in a crouching run. Longarm rose at the same time, fired, and Colonel Baxter somersaulted end-over-end to vanish once more in the sage. Longarm

176

threw two more rounds into the base of the resulting dust cloud and charged in the rest of the way, barefooted, to see if he'd hit the son of a bitch.

He had, he saw, as he found the colonel facedown in the cheat grass, vomiting blood and trying to breathe, with less luck. Longarm covered the dying man with his last two rounds as he moved on in, saying, "Morning. I don't suppose you'd like to tell me what this was all about before you finish dying, you sneaky prick?"

The colonel must not have. As he suddenly went limp all over Longarm sighed, hunkered down beside the body, and reloaded his six-gun from the other man's cartridge belt. Then he hurried back to where he'd left Peggy, lest someone come along and ask how come he was standing bare-ass in the sage with a smoking gun in one hand. As he rejoined her, he said, "It pains me to say it. But we'd best get dressed and pack Colonel Baxter into Vernon before the sun gets to work on him. We can make it by noon if we don't mind getting sweaty and almost as stinky."

She gasped, "Colonel Baxter? Why in God's name did you have to shoot *him*, darling?"

"He was out to shoot us. Me, at any rate. I don't know why, yet. He'll likely keep a few minutes if you'd like to make love again before we have to get going."

She protested that her passion was just ruined, for now, at least, and so he brushed sand and gravel off his bare skin and rejoined her on the bedroll as they both got dressed. She kept asking him what it all meant and he kept telling her he had no idea, explaining, "That's why I suggested making love some more. I fear that from here on it's likely to be more infernal paperwork than fun!"

Chapter 16

It wasn't that bad. Once they got into Vernon, as trail-dusty
and overheated as he'd promised, old Pop, the town law,
said he'd keep the colonel in a root cellar for now and that
Miss Peggy could use their jailhouse shower if she didn't
mind cold well water. She blessed him as a gentleman of
the old school and allowed she was ready, after that long
lope in the sun, to bathe in ice water. Longarm said he
might be by to scrub her back once he checked out the
telegraph office.

As he headed that way, old Pop caught up with him,
saying, "You must have been just funning. She didn't
strike me as that sort of a lady, you fresh rescal."

Longarm replied, "The kind of a lady she might be ain't
the mystery on my mind right now, Pop. Let's talk about
that well water she's splashing in right now."

The older lawman shrugged and said, "There's nothing
too mysterious about wells, Longarm. It's the only way to

get water this far out from the hills, unless you count that pissy brown stuff running down Cherry Creek right now."

Longarm said, "I've been spotting wind-pumped wells all the way north, along the basin of the Cedar Ranges."

Pop asked so what and Longarm said, "That means a fairly easy-to-get-at water table, under a sandy surface that won't hold water worth shit. So why would anyone want to dig dry ditches all over creation, when all they'd have to do would be to sink a mess of tube wells, cheaper?"

Pop shrugged and said, "If irrigating in these parts made much sense, the Mormons would have done so, long ago. Are you hinting that gent in the root cellar was flimflamming settlers with an irrigation scheme that wasn't practical?"

By this time they'd made it to the Western Union and as both breathed easier in the sudden shade, Longarm said, "He was up to something more sneaky than selling desert lots. He wasn't asking all that much and all the lots he sold already *have* water, if only you want to *drill* for it. The runoff from the Cedars keeps the water table under the sage flats fairly shallow. Hold the thought while I find out some more by wire."

The old man did. The first thing Longarm found was the message Billy Vail had sent some time back. Longarm read it, swore, and told Pop, "I've been hunting snipe, goddamn it!"

Pop asked, "Is that a snipe we just put in the root cellar?"

"In a way. My office sent me out to Vernal, not Vernon, for, ah, political reasons. This wire and money order says I should have been headed back to Denver by now."

"What about them mysterious night riders?" Pop asked.

Longarm sighed and said, "There weren't any. It was just a dumb excuse to get me out of Denver for a spell. My department didn't have any sensible reason to send me here to begin with."

179

"Then how come someone was so anxious to stop you?" the old man protested.

Longarm turned to the clerk on the far side of the counter and said, soberly, "I know you're not supposed to tell what others may or may not have sent through your private wires, old son. But to save us both a lot of bother I'd best tell you I've had this conversation before and, so far, I keep winning. Western Union's wires stretch across many a mile owned outright by the federal government, which I work for. So what's it going to be?"

The clerk shrugged and asked, "What do you want to know?"

Then, as he got digging into his files Longarm started to wire other lawmen in accordance with what he found. When it developed the late Handsome Luke had sent a sort of gibberish night letter to some pal called Scotty, in Reno, Longarm smiled wolfishly and wrote out a message to the federal marshal's office in Reno, requesting they pick up a gambling man called Linkletter on an attempted murder charge.

Then he explained, "The one as tried to push me off a train was a pimp traveling with a runaway orphan and a bad conscience. Linkletter is a Scotch name. Coming here, I cleaned out a crooked gambler who may have been called Scotty in code, and he said right out he was on his way to Reno. Passing through, say, Bingham Canyon, the sore loser hired Handsome Luke Harding to gun me. I'd made the mistake of letting Linkletter know I was bound for Vernon, even though it was the wrong place. When I showed up, later, on a pony Handsome Luke had stolen, a sidekick with a slower horse he'd left to wait for him tried to take revenge on me. Colonel Baxter had nothing to do with it. He yelled a warning out of simple charity and that takes care of that angle. The pissed-off gambler was the only crook those two were in with, see?"

"Not hardly," Pop said. "If that gent in the root cellar

180

didn't care if you was dead or alive, how did he wind up in the root cellar so dead?"

"That came later," Longarm said. "After I'd given him two good reasons, or so he thought. He suspected I might suspect him of gunning Badger Dawson over a gal they was both enjoying. I as much as called him a yellow dog to his face, and he knew I'd been talking to his wife, Lavinia, who kept telling anyone who'd listen that her man was fooling with a hussy in some way connected to the Last Gasp Saloon. With both men dead, we'll never know for sure whether Badger was blackmailing him or just telling him to stay clear of his woman. Since neither is a federal crime, it don't really matter, now."

Pop looked for a place to spit, didn't spot any, and swallowed before he said, "Going after a lawman who might or might not suspect you of fighting over women was sort of loco if you ask me."

"He may have had more serious motives," Longarm said. "Aside from saying things a guilty mind could have twisted into a sort of accusation, I told him right out I meant to look into the hard-rock mining background of old Omaha Orwell."

Pop frowned and said, "You just told us that saddle tramp was gunning for you on his lonesome, old son."

Longarm nodded and explained, "That was a guilty mind at work as well. The last thing Colonel Baxter wanted me looking into was hard-rock mining."

"How come? Did he have himself a mine?"

"Not yet. But he knew, or soon found out, I was riding out of his so-called irrigation scheme with a lady who could, if need be, likely draft me the whole layout from memory and a blank survey map. He wasn't trying to cheat anyone on sage flat property. He didn't give a hoot whether they made out there or not. The idea was to get control of a mess of canyons, he said, for the water rights. He was doing pretty good until I came on the scene to start asking questions that must have worried hell out of him. He'd suckered a mess of mountain settlers into swapping all their rights in the high country for flatlands as made about as much sense for crops or cows, and—"

"Thunderation!" Pop cut in. "The Cedars run down as a spur from them splendiferous hills along the south shore of the Great Salt Lake! What was he after, gold, silver, or copper?"

Longarm said, "We'll find out once we get some mining men in to survey. Whatever it was, he hadn't told even his hired help what he had in mind. He wanted it all sewn up, along with the water power needed, before he announced his strike. If you'd like an educated guess, I'd say it was placer gold. You need dams and a good headwater for a serious hydraulic operation. The few settlers up among the headwaters hadn't been pressured too hard. So we can assume the murderous old bastard *had* the claims he meant to change from water to mineral rights. He was ready to fend off rival mining claims by the time I arrived. It must have pissed him considerable when he thought I was on to him."

Pop started to ask a dumb question. Then he nodded and decided, "Nobody could have been in on it with him. No boss crook would've been dumb enough to come after you and that gal, personal, if he had anyone he could trust with the chore on his payroll. What happens to all them poor dupes now?"

Longarm shrugged and said, "For openers, I mean to see at least one sweet little Mormon gal and her man get their old canyon spread back. Deals made with a crook don't count, if anyone can charge fraud, and I mean to. The workers and the tinhorns living off them won't be hurt too bad. The colonel was paying well for useless play-acting. Settlers who bought land off IIT can still drill for water, even if we can't make Miss Lavinia give their down payments back to 'em. So let me get cracking with this pencil stub and I'll see how good I can patch things up for the innocent parties by wire."

He did. It didn't take long, but even so, Peggy Mason

was cleaned up and dried off by the time he got back to her. He told her to wait until he'd showered off and could ride on over to Lofgreen with her.

So three days later he showed up at the Denver federal building to catch holy hell from Billy Vail some more. He sat in the big leather guest chair while Billy war-danced around him for a spell, pointing at the banjo clock on the wall and saying mean things about Longarm's grasp of time and distance.

When at last even Billy Vail had to stop for breath Longarm flicked ashes on the rug, ground them in neatly with his boot heel, and said, "Don't get your bowels in such an uproar, boss. I wired you from Salt Lake that I had to tidy up the case with the territorial government and land management office."

Vail snapped, "That was days ago, damn it, and what did you mean by running up a hotel bill in the best hotel in Utah?"

Longarm looked innocent and said, "Oh, that was for a material witness who helped us sort some title deeds out. I told you about that, ah, draftsman in my first report."

"You did indeed," Vail said. "So how come you had to put that dead con man's draftsman up in a damned honeymoon suite?"

Before Longarm had to answer that, Henry came in with a wire from Washington, saying, "I took the liberty of opening this for you, sir. It seems the Interior Department's cited Longarm here for ending the career of a man who's done all sorts of dreadful deeds under a dozen different names."

Vail looked stunned, for just a second. Then he stuck out his chest and said, "Well, of *course* they had to congratulate us, damn it. When I send out one of *my* deputies I expect him to get his man, even when I don't know exactly where I sent him!"

Watch for

LONGARM IN THE BIG BURNOUT

one hundred and thirteenth in the bold
LONGARM series from Jove

LONGARM

Explore the exciting Old West with
one of the men who made it wild!

LONGARM

Explore the exciting Old West with one of the men who made it wild!